Submitting To Love

Sexy Stories Collection

VOLUME 1

6 EROTIC SHORT STORIES

CARRICE MCKELVY

Publisher's Note: This is a work of fiction. Names,
characters, places, and incidents are a product of
the author's imagination. Locales and public
names are sometimes used for atmospheric
purposes. Any resemblance to actual people, living
or dead, or to businesses, companies, events,
institutions, or locales is completely coincidental.

Submitting To Love/ Carrice McKelvy. -- 1st ed.
Xplicit Press, an imprint of TLM Media LLC

ISBN-13: 978-1-62327-523-5
ISBN-10: 1-62327-523-7
eISBN: 978-1-62327-582-2

Printed in the United States of America

CONTENTS

1 A LOVE–HATE RELATIONSHIP

When had she ever thought that being a journalist would be a good idea? She'd been working for Music Inc. for 6 months; she went to gigs and interviewed up and coming bands. It was hard to believe, but it was starting to get boring. How was that even possible? She met a large group of people so diverse that she'd probably have to check to see if they were even human. Some of these groups adopted personas, and they didn't come out of character for anyone.

Then there was her boss, James Berwick. He cut so many lines out of her copy she was starting to think he just liked using the red pen. From her cubicle, she could see his office. The tall, dark haired man was such a huge pain in her ass. It didn't help that he was good looking, because whenever she was around him, she got flustered. Somebody that sexy shouldn't be working as an editor at a music magazine. He should be on the papers advertised as a sex god with a mike.

"Are you daydreaming again?"

Georgina smiled at Keith over her shoulder. He mostly worked in the reviews department. He was handsome, too, but in a rather straight-laced kind of way; he'd once told her that he had met his fiancée at one of the gigs. Georgina had never met her, but it did evoke an interesting image. Keith dressed in a suit, and his soon-to-be wife wore God knows what. People had said that they were an odd pair, but Georgina already knew that they were happy. Keith never complained, and he always got this goofy look on his face whenever he talked about her.

"I was just wondering if I could kill James and get away with it." It wasn't a complete lie. Georgina had just received his latest revision on her article about a heavy rock band that was making the circuit. She handed the sheet of paper to Keith and he looked over it.

"Well, don't kill me, but he's right. You're a good writer, George, but some of this can be described as fluff. I think that you'd be ideally suited to features."

She nearly growled in frustration. "He's never going to let me write features. I'm starting to wonder if there's any point in staying here."

Her friend looked shocked. "You don't mean that."

She couldn't help the tired sigh that slipped from her lips. "I think I do. Come on, I think it's time for the weekly meeting. James is starting to pace in his office again."

Keith left her; there was no mistaking the worried look on his face. Georgina did her best to ignore it as she collected her pieces of paper. She'd already finished writing up the revisions and she'd emailed it to James's computer. She'd always wanted to be a writer; she knew that this opportunity was something people her age would kill for.

She finished collecting her things and headed off to James' office. It was time for the job assignments for the weekend.

Georgina didn't bother to rush; it hadn't been that long ago that she'd been the first person in the office. This writing job was her first, and she'd been eager to impress. For the last few weeks, she'd kept to the back of the small offices. She stayed quiet, didn't ask questions. This job was supposed to be fun, but it hadn't been for a long time.

She waited until a few of the other writers had gotten seated and then joined them. James was busy at his desk; it was always clean, and his secretary Lynda made sure that all the papers were filed away. Georgina was sure that without Lynda he'd be drowning under paper. He was dressed in his usual suit; she never saw him in anything vaguely casusal. He was tall, and the suit was incredibly well-fitted in a dark shade that caught the color in his eyes. The tie was the same shade as the suit, but it had been loosened at the neck; the top button of the white shirt was undone. The suit jacket had been hung up on the back of the door. From her seat at the back of the room, she was quite close to it, and the rich smell of his aftershave tickled at her nose.

Okay, she might hate him, but she wasn't dead from the waist down. He was good-looking, but the fact he was a complete asshole nine out of ten times kind of killed any attraction.

She half listened to the usual conversation; he talked sales and something about how he wanted to bring the company into the twenty-first century. When James then handed out the assignments, she started to pay closer attention. What in hell was he going to unleash on her today? Five articles on Greek throat music? Something she'd end up spending hours researching, only for him to unleash the red pen and then tell her that he doesn't need them after all.

The guy was an asshole.

She waited for a piece of white paper; everyone else had theirs, and she had nothing. James walked back to his desk. A few of the other journalists looked at her. Christ, was he going to fire her? He couldn't have just brought her into his office earlier, he had to humiliate her like this? She was tempted to chuck something at his head. She was sure that there was nothing in there to hurt, anyway. Everyone was starting to leave, and Georgina was tempted to join them. She might as well pack up her desk. She needed a stiff drink and a look at the job section of the paper.

She was just getting back to her feet when she heard James ask, "Georgina, can you stay for a second, please?"

There were a few looks of sympathy and she stopped in her steps. Well, it looked like she wouldn't just be able to leave without losing her temper.

She didn't look happy. He couldn't blame her; he could have told her about the change in assignments. Well, he could have but he chose not to. Georgina Grey had a lot of potential. She just didn't seem to want to tap into it. He'd tried to guide her; his methods a little heavy handed but that had usually worked so well in the past.

Keith had snuck in just before the meeting, slipped in a note onto his desk before he sat down. Georgina was thinking of leaving the company. He couldn't have that. She looked stressed, but she was dressed in a pale blue dress that kicked off at the hip, and it gave her a fresh look. She was young, inexperienced—maybe she needed a gentler touch? Which meant only one thing: he was going to have to take her under his wing. Give her a bigger assignment and see how she handled it.

"Are you firing me?"

He looked up into her angry green eyes. She really was quite pretty when she was upset; maybe, that was why he liked to see her get fired up and passionate. The thing was, she held onto her anger. It was frustrating.

"What gave you that impression?" She hadn't bothered to sit back down. It left him looking up at her, which he found annoying. "Why don't you sit down and we can talk?"

He was being reasonable. He wasn't known for being reasonable, and he could tell that it threw her. She didn't know how to react, and she lost some of the anger in her eyes. She sat down, crossing her legs at the ankle. The hem of her dress rode up slightly, and his eyes drifted down to the exposed length of thigh. She must have noticed his gaze; as she readjusted the dress, her cheeks were a faint shade of red. He'd made her blush, and it made her look younger. He'd made women blush before, but usually when there were fewer clothes involved and he had them in his bed. It was refreshing that he'd been able to do it to Georgina and he hadn't even said anything. All it had taken was a look.

"Are you firing me?" she asked again.

"Do you want to be fired?" Before she could answer, he continued, "You're a good writer, but I realize that I've been stifling you. Giving you smaller, irrelevant assignments hasn't worked. I wanted you to start at the bottom. We all had to when we came to this company, believe it or not, even me. Have you heard of Frankie Cartwright?"

"He was a singer with The Red Roses before he broke off and decided to become a solo artist."

"The record company is holding a showcase of their latest star; everyone will be there. You're going in to write me a feature on him."

She frowned. "Really?"

He sighed. "I'm not known for my sense

of humor. If I say that I want you to interview the guy, I mean it. The showcase is tomorrow night. Just be sure that I don't regret putting this much faith in you."

Georgina stood up, shock evident on her face. "Okay, it isn't a problem. I'll have the copy on your desk by Monday."

"You can meet me here tomorrow."

She stopped in her tracks again. "You want to give me a pep talk?"

"The showcase is in London. I've got two invites, so I'm not here to give you a pep talk. I'm going with you."

He didn't know where that came from. He'd had every intention of letting her go by herself, but he was oddly glad he was going. He'd finally be able to see the girl in action and figure out the best way to help her. James watched her, mostly out of the corner of his eye as she got her things together and left the office. When he was sure that he was the only one left, he removed his tie. With practiced ease, he threw it over the back of one of the chairs and then stretched out. After he'd managed to relax his strict posture, a rare smile graced his lips. He preferred it when the office was empty. He wore the suits because of the role he had to play. If he looked like the rest of the staff, then he might not have the same level of respect. The suits inspired a level of fear and respect that was essential as an editor of a busy magazine. With nimble fingers, he undid the shirt at the sleeves and rolled them up.

He had a copy to start putting together.

She knew that she should have felt excited about this; it was her big chance after all. The one event where she could prove to James she wasn't such a screw up. It was a little pathetic that even after he'd treated her like shit, she still wanted his approval.

Georgina walked across the road toward the building that housed the magazine and some other businesses. She didn't really know anything about them; sometimes, she'd meet some of them in the elevator, but they didn't talk, not really.

It had taken her forever to find something suitable to wear. She wanted to be professional but still have that edge of fun. This showcase was going to have a lot of important people there, but she doubted that they would all be wearing suits. In the end, she'd settled for a black wrap dress with a bold print on it. It gave the illusion of a professional, but showed off a lot of leg. Her long black hair had been braided and draped over her shoulder, and she wore the simplest of makeup. She looked good but not overdone.

There was also the fact that her delightful boss had decided to come with her, as if she wasn't under enough pressure already. The fact that he would be there, looking over her shoulder, was going to annoy the hell out of her.

Georgina figured that he'd probably be in the office, hard at work until the last minute. Tonight was going to be unbearable. She stepped into the lobby and promptly stopped. James was standing at the reception desk, talking to Amelia, the elderly woman who manned the desk, and he was smiling. She'd never seen him smile. Actually, she'd never seen him look so relaxed. He was wearing jeans that hung low on his hips. She couldn't see what shirt he was wearing, but it didn't matter. He was wearing a leather biker's jacket that fitted him beautifully.

Amelia smiled at her over his shoulder and James turned around, his smile breathtaking and unexpected.

"See you later, Lia," he said over his shoulder as he walked towards her. How could she have never noticed before? Of course, she knew that he was good-looking; she would have had to be blind not to have noticed. It was his attitude at work that was always so unattractive. Tonight, he was magnetic. This was nearly as bad as having him looking over her shoulder all night. If she had to stand close to him all night in a busy bar, she could just bury herself in his scent. In fact, she'd want to.

"You look nice," he said as he walked passed her and she dutifully followed him, muttering a thank you.

"Are we taking a car?" she asked as they walked towards the employee's parking lot.

He half smiled at her question. "I don't drive a car." It was then she saw it. It was the most beautiful vehicle she'd ever seen. The lines were sleek, the color a rich red. This motorcycle was sex on two wheels.

"Is this yours?" Georgina couldn't help stepping ahead of him and running her hand over the smooth body of the machine.

"Yes, it's an adapted Ducati originally built for off-road use. It's perfectly safe for two people." She watched as he unhooked two motorcycle helmets and handed her one.

She'd always wanted to own a motorcycle, because when she'd been younger, she'd been quite the thrill seeker. It was probably the product of being the only girl in a house full of boys. Her heart was beating so hard, she thought James could hear it. It wasn't just because she was about to ride this magnificent beast of a motorcycle. It was the fact that she was going to have to hold on tight to James. Her bare legs would hug him closely from behind. The thought made her wet with desire.

James straddled the motorcycle, flicked his hair back, and slipped the helmet on. Indecision tore at her; she couldn't start lusting after her boss. It was hardly her fault that she'd discovered hidden layers, and this more relaxed version of her boss was ticking all the boxes for her. She slipped the helmet on and got on behind him.

"You're going to want to put your hands around my waist."

She followed his instructions. It was only when he flicked a switch and the engine roared to life, she gave an almost inaudible moan of desire.

As they walked into the showcase, James had such a hard-on that he was surprised that it didn't affect his balance. The boxers that he wore were tight, and at the moment, as uncomfortable as hell. He was pretty sure that Georgina didn't know that he could hear her moan as they drove to the showcase. She had liked the motorcycle ride; she'd liked it a lot. He caught a glimpse of her face just after she removed her helmet and her eyes had been dark with desire.

There was something so sexy about it, a woman who loved his motorcycle. When he'd found time to go on dates, most of the women had wrinkled up their noses at his beloved bike and talked about how it must be a phase or a midlife crisis. Those dates had never gotten any further than that.

Georgina had loved it and that meant a lot to him. The added fact that the dress she wore was quite short meant her pussy had been pressed into his lower back. It hadn't helped the hard-on. It felt like a circle of intense heat. He wondered if it had just been the machine or the fact she was holding onto him. He dismissed that idea quickly. He knew she hated him; she was going to leave the company if he couldn't entice her to stay. He didn't want her to leave.

They quickly made the rounds around the showcase. James introduced her to a few people, and then they had to get in a line so they could interview Frankie in turn. They didn't talk much. It was hard to hear each other over the loud music of the support band. He watched as Georgina looked through her notes. Glancing up, she caught his gaze and leaned forward.

She was shorter than him, and he caught the scent of vanilla from her hair. She smelled good.

"Do you want to look at these? They're the questions I'm going to ask Frankie."

He took the notepad and looked it over. They weren't that bad. "Throw in a random question. All of these are good. A pretty girl asking him questions will probably boost his ego to no end. You might be able to find something out that will do wonders for your future."

She looked surprised. "Did you just call me pretty?"

He couldn't believe how that had slipped out. He'd always prided himself on his self-control. Somehow, Georgina always managed to slip under his defenses effortlessly. "It's time for you to head into the interview. Meet me at the bar when you're done."

The interview had gone well, so Georgina left the green room feeling quite pleased with herself. She found James standing at the bar with a drink in his hand, watching the band play. Frankie would be going up and playing his set as soon as the last journalists had asked their questions.

As she and Frankie had shaken hands, he'd slipped a piece of paper into hers and winked at her. It was only when she left that she found out it was his telephone number. Frankie was attractive, if not in the same league as her boss. She looked at James - who hadn't even noticed her yet - and back to the number in her hand.

Then she did the unthinkable; she threw away Frankie's number and walked to James. He smiled at her when he finally noticed her.

"How did it go?"

"Great. I'll type it up and I'll have it on your desk by Monday morning."

He nodded as he took a drink from his glass. He turned slightly and retrieved a glass from behind him. "I didn't know what you drink so I got you a white wine."

"Thanks." She smiled as she took it, "You didn't have to do that."

He looked a little sheepish. "Actually, I probably did. I've been a complete jerk to you, and I'm sorry. Let's take this as a peace offering."

Anger flared through her. "Are you telling me that you gave me this assignment because you felt sorry for me?"

"Why are you angry? I wanted you to stay at the company. I knew that I was treating you like an ass and I knew that you deserved better."

"Well I'll tell you what, James, you can just go and fuck yourself. I don't need your fucking pity assignments. I quit."

She stormed out of the bar, quickly downing her drink before she left. She thought that James had changed, but he was really just a manipulative bastard. Her heels echoed loudly in the street.

"Georgina, wait," a familiar voice called out somewhere behind her. "Georgina, let me at least give you a ride home."

She spun on her heels and waited for a flustered James to catch up. "Why have you been such an ass to me? Since day one, you've delighted in driving me insane, and now, today, you decide you want to be a nice guy. What the hell happened?"

He grabbed her roughly by the shoulders and pulled her towards him. The move was so sudden that she didn't try to pull away. His lips crashed down on hers in a kiss that would leave her lips swollen and bruised. She could taste the alcohol on his breath. He wasn't drunk, she knew that, it was the only reason she didn't pull away. She'd spent the majority of her time hating him, but it wasn't hate that was growing in the pit of her stomach, it was desire. The kiss seemed to go on forever before she finally broke it. "I'll still quit you know."

The smile that graced his lips was utterly male. "That works. With what I want to do to you, I can't if you work for me."

His words left her breathless. "And what do you want to do with me?"

He drove her to a secluded spot. The moon was full in the sky and cast everything in a pale white glow. She'd barely been able to stop herself from playing with his hard cock as he steered the motorcycle. It was dangerous and reckless but she didn't care. She wanted to feel his hard cock in her hand. The throbbing of the machine between her legs was driving her insane with desire. He stopped, kicked out the stand on the bike, and started to kiss her. She loved the feel of his hands on her. He reached for the bow that held the dress together and pulled it; cool air bathed her body making her nipples rock hard.

She was practically dripping wet, and as he hooked his thumbs into the band of her panties, pulling them down, he buried his head deep into the gap between her legs. His tongue flicked out, and he gently bit on her clit.

There was something incredibly freeing about doing this outside; there weren't any houses around, nobody for miles. It only seemed like seconds, and she was already calling out his name, coming over his face. He looked up, the light of the moon catching his devilish grin, and he wiped a hand across his jaw.

"Damn, you taste good."

He kissed her again, and she could taste her juices on his lips. He gently touched her breasts, and she leaned back against his motorcycle. It felt like a dream, and she wondered if she should pinch herself. She was really having sex with her boss on his motorcycle.

When she'd quit previous jobs, it had never ended up like this.

"What do you want me to do to you?" he asked in a low voice.

"I want you to bend me over this beautiful machine and fuck me from behind." The words left before she could stop them, and she watched as her boss's eyes looked at her approvingly. She turned around, spread her legs, and raised the skirt of her dress up and over her hips. Her panties were already off, so at least she didn't have to worry about taking them off.

"I can't tell you how much I've wanted to do this." He touched her ass, a smooth circle on each cheek before giving it a gentle tap.

"Fuck me or fuck somebody on this bike?" she whispered back at him.

"Both."

He undid his jeans, pulling them down to his knees. His cock was rock hard, standing straight and proud. He ran his hand up and down it a few times and the head glistened with precum. He ripped open the condom packet and rolled the condom on in one practiced sweep.

James put a hand on her hip and rubbed the head of his cock against the opening of her wet pussy. Her whole body shook with desire and she moaned loudly. He wanted to feel her wet folds over his dick so badly, but he knew that if he rushed this he'd be coming so fast that it would be a waste.

He reached around and found her clit again, using his thumb to play with it and she cried out. Her pussy was gushing with juices; this was probably turning her on as much as him.

"Please, James," she gasped.

"Please what, Georgina?"

"I need you to fuck me. I need to feel your cock inside of me now." Her voice was thick with desire.

"How do you want it?"

"I want it as fast and as hard as you

can give it."

"That sounds like a challenge." He grabbed his cock and angled just above her wet hole. With a swift pump of his hips, his cock was buried deep in her pussy. The shock of it made him pause. She felt so good and she was moaning as she rubbed her clit against the warm steel of the motorcycle. He wasn't going to last long but it didn't matter. He started to fuck her in long, slow thrusts. Her pussy clenched around his cock as he buried his cock to the hilt with each thrust inside her. They both shuddered at the sensation of each thrust; she was so tight.

"Faster, please James."

Those words were the only encouragement that he needed. His hips moved faster and faster, plowing in and out, in and out. She was going crazy underneath him; he lost count of how many orgasms that she'd had. It felt like her body had hit the crest of a wave, and she was staying up high. He was going to come soon.

He knew that moment was coming, his balls got unbelievably tight, and his mind went blissfully blank. It seemed to go on forever, and then it felt like he'd become boneless. He leaned over her body. "That was fucking incredible."

She laughed as they pulled apart and he took the condom off. "You know, I don't think I've ever heard you swear before."

"You must bring it out of me. We should start heading back."

Georgina readjusted her dress, tying it back up. "You want to drop me off at my place?"

"No, I think we should head back to mine and spend the weekend in bed. What do you say?" He held his breath. They'd just had sex on his motorcycle; it pretty much blew apart their working relationship even if she hadn't quit.

She took a few steps towards him. "I think that's an amazing idea," she said as she kissed him on the lips.

They had spent the entire weekend in bed, only leaving it so they could get the food that had been delivered. It had been incredible; they'd had sex everywhere. They'd managed to work their way through five boxes of condoms. They'd had sex in the living room, on the stairs, in the kitchen, in the bathroom twice, and finally in a bed, where they'd promptly fallen asleep. It had been amazing, and she fully intended to take advantage of this for however long it lasted.

When they weren't having sex, they'd been talking. They actually had things in common; she never would have guessed. They both loved motorcycles and ended up talking about the first ones that they'd owned. She'd studied his music, and they had a few of the same albums. If they hadn't stumbled into being lovers, if she hadn't worked for him, they would have met under different circumstances. They could have been friends. They didn't talk about the fact she'd quit. It didn't seem important now. If she had to choose between her job and being with him, she would have chosen him; in fact, it really wasn't even a choice.

It was Sunday night, James had fallen asleep an hour ago and it left Georgina with her thoughts. She wondered if they could have a relationship or if she should take this for what it could be. It had been a great weekend of sex, where nothing seemed to matter outside of these four walls. Did she want something more from him?

"You still awake?"

His voice startled her. "I thought that you were asleep."

"What are you thinking about?" He rolled onto his side, and she could see the outline of his body.

"Just about tomorrow. I'm going to have to start looking for another job."

"You can stay at the magazine if you want."

"That's probably not a good idea. I'll never be able to think straight in the same room as you, especially after this weekend."

"There is actually a new project that I'm talking to the business partners about. It's another magazine. You could write for that one if you want. It will have a new editor, which means that we won't be working together."

The idea was tempting. "I'll think about it."

He edged closer and pulled her into the crook of his arm. "I also think that we should go on a proper date. You want to grab dinner and a movie tomorrow night?"

"That sounds really good." It was an odd way to start a relationship, but she'd had a lot worse. She listened as James fell back to sleep and closed her eyes.

If somebody had told Georgina that she would end up having the best sex of her life with a man that she'd wasted a lot of time hating, she would have laughed. But maybe, people were right; there was really a thin line between love and hate.

2 NEVER LETTING GO

There were a lot of things Claudia Donovan might have expected to happen that day, pigs flying outside in the noon breeze or maybe even hell freezing over. The last thing that she expected was answering the front door and seeing Drew Carter standing on her doorstep, with bags at his feet. She fought the urge to step past him and check for winged pork soaring in the sky.

"Hey Dia," her high school crush and ex best friend greeted her. She didn't know if she wanted to hit him or hug him. She settled on standing in the doorway, her jaw practically hitting her chest. She hadn't seen him in ten years. It was like a flash to the past, he hadn't changed at all. His brown hair was still a little too long; the hair brushed the top of his earlobes. The blue eyes that had always managed to make her heart skip a beat in high school were still having the same effect on her now. "Drew, what the hell are you doing on my doorstep?"

He blushed. "I need to ask a pretty big favor."

How many times had she dreamed of a moment like this? Over the last few years, she'd thought about him a few times. He'd even taken a leading role in some of her fantasies. If she was actually dreaming he'd be taking her into his arms, pushing her against the wall and kissing her with those soft lips of his. She was midway into her fantasy when Drew reached out and pinched her arm.

"Ouch. What did you do that for?"

He shrugged. "You got that look you used to get in high school and while it's nice to see you, I really want to get out of the rain."

"I'll put the kettle on."

That night ten years ago seemed like a lifetime ago. Claudia had sworn to herself that she would never forgive Drew; actually, she thought she'd threaten him with a frying pan. It had been a crazy night. They'd both decided not to go to prom and that they would spend the night together watching bad movies and eating too much popcorn.

Then she'd turned up at his house just in time to see him leaving with Valerie Simpleton, all dressed up in a suit that had made him heartbreakingly gorgeous. He had the decency to look a little embarrassed and he said he was sure that she'd forgive him, eventually. Like hell she had. They hadn't talked much over the last ten years, but since Claudia's mom was friends with his, she still managed to get regular updates.

Not that she wanted them, much.

Now she had him sitting in her small kitchen, drinking a cup of hot chocolate. Claudia didn't keep tea or coffee in the house. They hadn't said anything yet. They just sat on opposite ends of the table, looking at each other. It reminded Claudia of a scene in an old western. Any minute now they'd pull out guns and shoot each other. She really couldn't believe that he was actually here.

"Are you planning on staring at me all night?"

"I can't believe that you're actually here," she replied honestly. "Why are you here?"

"I need a place to stay for a while. I've got some work lined up in London but hotel prices in this city are ridiculous. I'll pay you rent."

"Wait a minute," Claudia said, raising her hands, as if to stop him from saying any more. "You want to stay here, in this house, with me?"

He grinned and Claudia was thankful

that she was sitting down. She'd seen the effect of that devastating smile on unsuspecting girls during senior year. "Unless you'd want to move out for a while."

"How the hell did you even know that I was here?"

"Your mom told me. She also said to tell you that she'll call over the weekend."

She was going to kill her mother. After all this man had put her through, her mother practically pointed him in the direction of her home. She'd thought that she'd been pretty clear about not wanting to see Drew ever again. She watched as he rolled up the sleeves of his pullover, revealing tanned forearms. Damn, he looked really good. It was awful that he still had this effect on her, but the way he bit his bottom lip left her wondering how soft they were.

"Fine," she heard herself say. "You can stay but don't expect me to look after you."

He grinned again and went to collect his bags from the hallway. Claudia's eyes drifted down by their own accord to his ass, where his jeans fitted him perfectly. Damn, she thought, if I'm not careful I'm going to be in serious trouble.

She hadn't changed at all; she still had that spitfire which always used to make him smile. Her red hair was a lot shorter, and it had a wave to it that Drew had never noticed before. This wasn't a good plan. Actually, as far as plans went, this one was pretty stupid. But ten years ago, he had made a stupid mistake, and he'd regretted it ever since.

It had taken a considerable amount of skill and charm to get her mom to part with her address. Their heart-to-heart over coffee had set the record straight. He'd known that he'd made a terrible mistake but he'd been just a kid, scared about the way he felt about his best friend. Plus he was a boy — it was only as he left the house that night with Valerie and he'd seen his best friend's heartbroken expression, that he'd realized that Claudia had felt more than just friendship. And that he did, too.

Life had pulled them apart. Well, that and Claudia refusing to speak to him had played a massive part. From the updates his mom gave him, he'd known that Claudia hadn't been in a serious relationship about anyone else. Now it was going to take some of his best skills and a few dirty tricks to make Claudia understand he wanted to be with her. This might take a while, he thought, as he unpacked his bags.

The knowledge that Drew was asleep just across the hall had kept Claudia up for most of the night. When she'd eventually managed to fall asleep, she could hear birds starting to sing outside. This exhaustion was why, when she woke up a couple hours later, she'd completely forgotten about Drew moving in. That was, until she saw him standing in the kitchen, making something to drink, in just a pair of tight fitting blue boxers.

With his back to her, Claudia checked him out. He was still in pretty good shape, his body toned and tanned. Her tiny kitchen had never felt cramped before. She suddenly wished that she wasn't wearing her pajamas with teddy bears on them. He looked as sexy as hell, she really didn't compare.

It felt like her feet had suddenly grown roots. She couldn't move, she couldn't even drag her eyes away. Drew turned around, his eyes widening in surprise.

"You're awake early."

"I couldn't sleep." She didn't say that it was mostly his fault.

"Well I was going to knock on your door, tell you that I've made hot chocolate."

She walked to the kitchen table and sat

down. She was trying really hard not to stare but it was a battle that she was losing. Drew sat down opposite her again, still only in a pair of boxes, his hair messy from sleeping. Nobody should look that good; there should be a law against it. Claudia thought stubbornly, Damn, I can't sit here and make polite conversation when all I want to do is jump his bones. This is so unfair. "I'm going to have to drink this in my room."

Drew frowned. "Why? Is something wrong?"

"Of course not," she lied before quickly vanishing to the safety of her room.

She's always been such a terrible liar, Drew thought as he watched her leave. His body had gotten really hot under her eyes. He knew that appearing half naked in the kitchen was a low blow, but he was working under a deadline. He couldn't draw this out over months, with careful seduction. At this rate, she'd probably try and kick him out at the end of the week.

She must have been thinking of something pretty intense because her cheeks had gone a faint shade of red. She'd pretty much looked everywhere but his face. Phase one is complete, he thought, and I'm pretty sure that whenever she sees me now, she's going to be picturing this moment.

Drew didn't see Claudia again until

much later. He was pretty sure that she was avoiding him. She spent a lot of time in the basement and asked him not to bother her. He already knew that the basement was where she did the majority of her painting. She created the front covers of romance novels. Her work was so popular that she could afford the tiny house in London by herself. He tried to entice her to join him for dinner but she just shouted up that she was too busy and that she'd find something later. He pretty much resigned himself to the fate that he was going to have to try harder to see her.

Frustrated by the lack of success, he climbed back into bed and went to sleep. He wasn't sure how long that he'd been asleep when he heard the scream. He leapt out of bed and rushed toward the sound, following it to the basement and saw a dark shape lying on the ground. He flipped on the switch and the basement flooded with bright light.

"Claudia!" He took the steps two at a time and jumped down the last three. "Claudia, are you okay? What happened?"

She rolled onto her back. "I slipped on the last step, knocked my head and ended up on my ass. That teaches me for trying to navigate this place in the dark."

"Why were you in the dark?" He knelt down, he saw her eyes widen in surprise about his lack of clothes as he helped her sit up.

"There are two light switches. I didn't realize how late it was, so when I switched the light off down here, everything went dark. I thought that I would be all right but apparently not." Drew put his arm around her shoulders and helped her back to her feet. She felt incredibly light. Putting a hand to her cheek, he checked her eyes.

"Do you need to go to the hospital?"

"No." Her voice fluttered slightly, and he saw a blush rise to her cheeks.

They were so close that Drew could brush his lips against hers in a heartbeat. He couldn't do it now, though. She was probably in shock and even if she didn't think she needed to go to the hospital, he probably should take her anyway. He was still thinking this when she kissed him.

This really isn't a good idea, Claudia thought as she brushed her lips against Drew's. He made it quite clear ten years ago that he only viewed her as a friend. Her heart raced as Drew groaned, and he pulled her tightly against his body. She wrapped her arms around him, feeling his hard body under her hands. His hands were in her hair, holding her in place as he seemed to take control of the kiss.

Despite her body's longing, she pulled away from him. "I shouldn't have done that."

"I'm glad that you did."

She couldn't have been more shocked if he'd told her that the world was going to end. "You're glad of what?"

He stepped closer. "I'm glad that you kissed me."

"Oh God, how hard did I hit my head?" She had to be imagining this. He reached up and pushed her hair aside. His fingertips seemed to leave a trail of heat in their wake. He ran his fingers through her hair, lightly touching the back of her head checking for bumps. She closed her eyes as he touched her. She was worried that if he saw the desire in her eyes that they would end up doing more than kiss.

"I can't feel any bumps," he said, studying her face.

"You see, I'm fine." She struggled to keep her voice steady.

"Except for the fact you kissed me."

She opened her eyes and noticed that he was tantalizingly close to her. She could just reach out and touch that flat stomach, reach down and touch something even harder.

"You said that you didn't mind," she reminded him.

He smiled down at her. "I didn't. How about we go out tomorrow?"

This wasn't an easy conversation to have with a half-naked man whose lips made her melt. She fought the urge to step back into his arms, hook her thumbs into the waistband of his boxers and pull them off. She wanted to touch that nice, firm ass. She wanted to nibble it.

"Out where?"

"On a date, so we can get to know each other again."

Just the thought of his hands on her body was making her wet with desire. This was going to involve putting her heart on the line, but maybe she could keep lust and love separate? Could she just use and abuse him? Could she be that kind of girl?

"Okay, I've got to go to an art gallery thing tomorrow and check out the space for my show. Come with me and we can go out to lunch."

Drew's eyes seemed to sparkle with mischief. "That sounds perfect."

He never thought that he could be that strong. That kiss had nearly made him rock hard. Even though he'd waited ten years for that, it had been worth the wait. All he'd wanted to do was pull her to the ground and show her what ten years of sexual frustration had done to him. He'd be lucky if he lasted more than a minute.

Drew lay in his bed. The memory of the kiss was still fresh in his mind. His cock twitched. It demanded his attention and he reached down and pulled down his boxers. His cock sprung free, rock hard. He stifled a groan as he closed his eyes, imagining that it was Claudia's hand instead of his.

He slowly stroked his cock, imagining that he was being engulfed by Claudia's soft, pink lips; her looking up at him innocently while she sucked on him. A groan escaped his lips as he gripped a nearby pillow with his other hand. Drew clenched his jaw, hoping that it'd stop him from making too much noise, but staying quiet was hard as he felt the delicious pressure building and building.

His fantasy shifted and this time, Claudia was on top of him with her knees on his sides. She was gripping his cock as if to steady it, positioning it at the entrance of her pussy. But what turned him on even more was the image of Claudia's eyes filled with lust as she rode his cock. Drew started pumping faster as more images of Claudia played in his mind.

"Fuck!" he said in a harsh whisper as he was hit with a flash of pleasure. His toes curled and uncurled themselves as he came all over his hand, stomach, and all over the bed.

Panting heavily, Drew finally opened his eyes and assessed the mess he made. He sighed. "Now how am I going to explain this?"

Last night felt like a dream, a beautiful if slightly painful dream. Claudia couldn't believe that she'd kissed him, couldn't believe that she'd said yes to a date. She stood in front of her wardrobe and tried to pick out something that would both be suitable for a date and the gallery. The last time she'd been on a date, which had been about a year ago with a man called Derek, she'd bought a black dress. She wore it once and had forgotten about it. But now, she dug it from the back of her closet and slipped it on, smiling at herself in satisfaction. The black dress was professional enough to meet with a client, provided she coupled it with a long woolen cardigan, and sexy enough for a date if she wore it alone.

She picked up a pair of heels in her favorite color, a very sexy red, and quickly got ready.

When she finally walked into the art gallery, she knew that she'd made the right choice in outfits. Drew groaned as he looked at her. "Do you want to make it to see the client?" he asked in a low, throaty voice.

She looked at him with wide-eyed innocence, twirling on the spot and pretending to study her outfit. "What do you mean?"

Drew stalked towards her, stopping an inch away. "The fact is, you look so hot that all I want to do is to take you to the bedroom and do things to you that would make your eyes roll back in your head."

Despite the tremor of heat rushing through her body, she smiled sweetly at him. "You better keep your hands to yourself or the date is off."

Suppressing a growl of frustration, he saluted. "Yes, ma'am."

He could barely keep his eyes off her. He wondered if she realized how graceful she was talking about her art. The way her body moved had him mesmerized. He loved seeing her in her element.

At the same time, he couldn't stop wondering how their date would end. He wanted her body underneath his. He needed to hear her call out his name as their bodies became slick with sweat, as they explored each other.

"Are you okay?" she asked.

He blinked. He had no idea how long she'd been watching him. Had she asked him a question? The owner of the studio had disappeared and left just the two of them standing in the clear space. Claudia had said that the show was in a few days and then hopefully the tiny space would be packed.

"I'm fine," he lied. Judging by the look

she was giving him she knew that he was lying to her. "Okay," he amended, "I'm not. I want you so bad that I'm getting hard just thinking about it."

She looked at him as if she had no idea what he was talking about. "Really?" she replied, her voice faint with disbelief. "You want me that badly?"

Drew reached out and took her hand, brushing it against his growing cock. Her eyes widened in surprise, and then instantly darkened with desire. "I want you so bad that I would make love to you, right here and now."

"I don't think the manager would like that," she half joked, though he could tell the idea tempted her.

"Believe me, you wouldn't be focused on anyone else but me and what I would be doing to you."

She stepped closer. "And what would you be doing to me?"

He groaned as he caught the scent of her perfume, a vanilla musk that should have been innocent but was far from it. He still had a hold on her hand, though it wasn't resting on his crotch anymore. He pulled her towards him, fighting the urge to kiss her because he knew that if he did, he wouldn't be able to stop. Suddenly their bodies were touching, from chest to hip. He would have been surprised if you could fit anything between them. Drew dipped his head slightly, brushing her ear with his lips.

"I want to feel your breasts under my hands, play with your nipples with my fingers and my tongue. I'd kiss my way down and use my tongue on your body in a way that would make you scream. I would make you come again and again. Then when you start to beg for it, I'd make love to you all night long. That, I promise. I have ten years to make up for and I've been thinking about this a very long time."

He looked into her eyes. She was breathing heavily, and probably imagining everything that he'd said.

"I think we should leave now," she said breathlessly.

"You want to go to lunch?"

She shook her head. "No, I want to go home and I want you to make good on that promise."

They barely made it through the front door before they started to pull at each other's clothes. The need was incredible. Claudia had had other lovers before, but there had never been this overpowering need. Drew was right when he said that he had to make up for ten years, and she felt it too. It felt like the world's longest courtship and that she'd spent half that time pretending not to be interested in him.

The kiss in the basement was a pale shadow compared to this. The kisses were hard, buttons were lost and she thought that she broke the zipper on his jeans, but God, it was worth it. He might have tantalized her with the idea of slow and gentle love making but the day was young, and they had plenty of time for that. All she knew was she would go insane if he wasn't inside of her within the next 30 seconds.

He reached up her skirt for her panties and she smiled as he groaned against her lips. "You haven't been wearing any panties all day?"

"You really want to talk now?" she asked in mock disbelief.

"Hell, no." He picked her up and she wrapped both of her legs around his waist. He turned her so her back was pressed hard against the wall.

"I hope you're ready for the best sex of your life," Drew whispered in her ear before thrusting hard, planting himself deep inside her. He felt her fingernails scrape his neck and her other hand had a firm grip on his hair. But the pain only added to the pleasure he felt. It felt so good to be inside her, to hear Claudia moan his name over and over again like a prayer. How long had he waited for this moment? How many times had he jerked off thinking about making love to Claudia?

His train of thought was broken as Claudia kissed him hard. "Oh, D—Drew," she moaned loudly, "I—I'm coming."

He quickened his thrusts as he, too, felt his climax drawing near. "Go ahead, baby," he said. "Let it all out."

And that's exactly what Claudia did, screaming in pleasure as she writhed against him. Drew came after three more thrusts, pulling his cock from her to shoot his semen all over her dress.

They settled down on the floor with their arms still around each other as Claudia laughed. "Wow, now I know what it's like to see stars."

Drew rested his head on her shoulder. "I'm so sorry."

She sighed happily. "What are you talking about? That was pretty damn amazing. And don't worry about the dress; I didn't like it anyway."

He shook his head. "It's not that. I wanted our first time to be special."

His words touched her heart. She laced her fingers with his. "Come on, let's go take a shower."

In the bathroom, Drew took his time helping Claudia to get undressed. She giggled at the attention, but Drew didn't mind. He'd imagined her body a hundred different ways, and now he finally had it under his hands. She was smooth and soft. As his fingers travelled over her skin, she giggled and then moaned with desire. She danced away from him and he loved the way her hips swayed as she turned around and switched the shower on.

"God, you're beautiful."

She stopped, looking over her shoulder at him and winked. "Are you planning to take off your clothes or do you want to come in fully dressed?"

Drew didn't need to be told twice; he stripped off his clothes and stumbled around a bit as he pulled off his socks. He'd never been this nervous before. The wild tumble in the hallway had taken off some of his desperate need but he was quickly becoming hard again. He could go another round. Hell, he could probably go another two.

God, Claudia thought, if this is a dream I don't think I ever want it to end. She turned on the shower, put a hand under the hot stream to make sure that it wasn't too hot and stepped under the water. Her body felt sore in a good way. They'd waited for so long; it shouldn't have felt that good. She felt the water pour over her breasts and she looked seductively at Drew.

"You want to get in here with me, or are you just going to watch?"

He stepped under the water with her. She was under no illusions that they were actually going to get clean. Not by the way Drew turned her around or how he cupped her breasts and the way his heavy erection rested against her butt.

They had sex several times that night; it had felt like he was committing every inch of her body to memory. It was only after he'd gone down on her that she had to put a stop to it. Her body couldn't take anymore. He pulled her into the crook of his body and had promptly fallen asleep. Claudia might have been tired but her body just wouldn't follow suit.

After an hour, she finally got up and dressed in a worn pair of leggings and a cozy top. What a strange day, she thought as she made her way to the kitchen. It wasn't like she was complaining, since she'd just had the best sex of her life. Drew had lived up to every teenage fantasy, in every possible delicious way. She brewed a cup of coffee and sat in the quiet kitchen.

Soon it would be all over, since there was no way he would stay now. This had been a huge mistake, a wonderful mistake, but it didn't matter. She thought that she could have been objective about it but she knew if Drew stayed, she'd fall in love. She wouldn't be able to help herself. There was still a part of her that wasn't sure if he felt the same way that she did. Was this all just a coincidence? Had it only happened because he was staying with her? Was he playing with her feelings?

Anger went through her and she swallowed it down. This was her choice, she was an adult, and maybe she should just accept this for what it was, a chance to revisit the past and do things differently.

Just because they'd slept together – well, not slept – but had mind-blowing sex together didn't mean that they were going to get together. She retrieved a piece of paper and quickly wrote a note. It came out colder than she would have liked but it got the point across. It would be easier for everyone involved if Drew left in the morning. She didn't regret what happened between them, but there was no way they'd ever be able to go back to being just friends. She'd be out for most of the day and she wanted him gone by the time she got back. She signed her name and then got ready to leave. Thankfully, they'd ended up his bed last night so she didn't have to worry about being quiet enough.

She was gone by the time he woke up. He didn't even have to get out of his room to know that she wasn't in the house. He put his hand onto her side of the bed and noticed that it was cold. Last night had left him exhausted; he couldn't believe that they'd lost years due to his own stupidity.

He quickly got dressed and searched the house. He found the note on the kitchen table and as he read it, he laughed. He knew that she would do this. Last night had been perfect, so it made some twisted kind of sense that she would be running scared. Ten years ago it had been him who'd been sent running.

Drew took his phone out of his pocket and dialed. It didn't take long to find out where she might be from her mother. It sounded like Claudia had a studio in the city and if she'd gone anywhere, it would be there. He thanked her and then went to his bedroom. He knew exactly where to find the box.

"You do know I love you, right?"
Claudia had been in her own little world

when she heard Drew's unmistakable voice. She spun around in surprise. "How the hell did you find me here?"

"Your mom," Drew said with a smile as he walked towards her.

He heard her briefly mutter something about killing her mother and she stopped, a shocked expression dawning on her face. The words had finally sunk in. "You love me?"

"Of course I love you. I've loved you for years and I was just too blind to see it. This isn't just a one night stand for me, Dia." He walked towards her and reached into his pocket. "I knew you hated me or at least thought that you did. I had to be sure that this would work before I did something I couldn't take back."

She looked confused and Drew couldn't blame her. "What are you talking about?"

He bent down and in one smooth movement pulled out the box. He watched as Claudia's eyes went impossibly wide, and he flipped open the velvet box, revealing the ring inside. "Claudia Donovan, will you marry me?"

She fell to her knees and kissed him. "Yes, I will."

At that moment, Drew felt like he could die with a smile on his face. He stood up and spun Claudia round and round, making her laugh. It was when he set her down that she put her arms around his neck, stood on her toes, and kissed him hard on the lips, pressing her breasts against his chest.

Drew caught on quickly and felt himself growing hard. He lifted her up again and walked to a long table where he sat her down. He broke the kiss only long enough to take off his clothes while she took off hers. This was different from their lovemaking last night, when their hearts were still hidden out of fear of rejection. But the fear was finally gone after ten long years. Now, they had nothing to hide.

Claudia lay down on the table with Drew on top of her, his weight pressing deliciously on her as they kissed softly. She felt the tip of his cock against her entrance, teasing her, making her yearn for Drew's hardness. Feeling frustrated, Claudia wrapped her legs around his waist and tried to thrust herself onto his cock, but to no avail.

He smiled against her lips as he finally gave in to her wishes. He entered her slowly, reveling in the feeling of Claudia's tight mound squeezing him inch by inch. She moaned at the feel of him inside her, slowly moving in and out. She held onto him tightly as he moved faster and faster, bringing them both to the edge.

They came at the same time as they shuddered at the intensity of their orgasms. He collapsed on top of her, both of their chests heaving.

"I love you," Drew whispered, looking into Claudia's eyes. She could hear all the love he had for her in his voice and it made her eyes well up.

"I love you, too," she replied, smiling. "But don't think this means you're off the hook."

Drew laughed and kissed her forehead. "Don't worry; I will still make it up to you. All ten years of it."

"Really?"

"Even if it takes the rest of our lives together."

3 REMEMBERING HOW TO LOVE

In their ten years of being together, Henry couldn't get enough of his wife. The feel of her white skin under his hands, the way she moaned as he played with her. That wetness between her legs drove him wild. He always focused on her first, playing with fingers and then his tongue. He loved the taste of her against his lips.

After she'd come a few times, the wetness became so slick and hot that he knew sinking into her was going to feel amazing. He loved the way she moaned into his ear as he positioned himself between her legs, the way that she wrapped her legs around his waist. Her hooded eyes seemed to demand that he finish what he started. Henry knew how lucky he was to have a wife who challenged him and made him laugh on a regular basis. When he pushed into her, the feeling of tightness and the wetness of her pussy around his throbbing cock always nearly undid him then and there. Her spine would arch as he slowly worked himself in and out of her wet hole. She would scrape her nails down his back and hiss as if the size of him hurt her in a good way.

It was always what she did next that would drive him completely crazy. "I want you to fuck me as hard as you can." A breathy whisper in his ear; a sort of permission. Then he would pound, thrust, and play with her. He wanted, needed to feel her come around his cock.

When she did, his mind went blissfully blank and he'd start to breathe heavily. He could never remember saying anything at that point, and he didn't care. It was only afterwards that she would tell him how much it turned her on, enough for her body to fall back into orgasm as if being hit by a crest of a wave, when he started to speak.

"I'm going to come now baby, oh my God, you feel so good."

It was after one afternoon of absolutely blinding sex that everything changed.

Henry Docking sat in the chair next to the hospital bed and studied his sleeping wife's face. Rachel looked so peaceful, her blonde hair, which had been brushed in her sleep, fanned out slightly. The effect made her look like a sleeping princess. He only wished that it would just take a kiss to wake her up.

The hospital machines beeped in time with her pulse. He'd spent every waking hour and most of his sleeping hours with her. He'd become used to the sound. The thought was depressing. The accident had happened two weeks ago. It was almost like she'd been frozen in time and the world was trying to move him forward. He didn't want to move forward, though; he wanted time to go back. He wanted for the argument not to happen. They argued so rarely that when they did it got explosive, but they still never should have gotten behind the wheel in anger. It had been tempting fate. Then that damn rabbit had darted into the road and instead of slamming on the brakes, Henry had swerved. The force of hitting the tree had thrown both of them forward. The airbag on his side had opened. Rachel's hadn't.

The doctors had run all sorts of tests; she had been concussed when her head hit the windshield. They said it was probably the shock and pain that caused her to slip into a coma. Her brain was trying to repair itself. It sounded a little farfetched to him, but he'd needed something to cling on to.

He reached out, picking up her hand. Limp and lifeless, if it wasn't for the beeping equipment and the fact her hand was warm... Well, he didn't want to dwell on it. He brought her hand to his lips, feeling the stubble brush her skin. He hadn't bothered shaving, and he didn't want to leave just in case that was the moment that she woke up. She would be terrified to wake up alone in a hospital.

One of the nurses came in, but he barely looked at her. He knew that there was going to be a time soon that they'd make him leave. Not because they didn't understand his situation, but because as the hours and the days ticked by, the hope that she would wake up was slipping away.

"Any change to our sleeping beauty?" She checked the machines.

"No," he replied. Honestly, he couldn't help the intense feeling of guilt that swept over him. This was worse than her simply dying. If she'd died in the accident then he could grieve. He couldn't say goodbye to her, and he didn't want to, not when there was a chance that she might wake up. He loved his wife, but this was torture to him.

He was dreaming. It was a restless sleep with fractured dreams. Rachel was screaming at him, the rabbit with impossibly large eyes looming from the darkness. As the car bumped down the hill, it was like everything was in slow motion. He wanted it to stop but his dream self didn't know the end. He couldn't see the tree as it drew closer.

Henry watched the action unfold from the back seat, a passenger in his own nightmare. He wondered how much of it was true. Had he really looked at Rachel, reaching out to grab her hand the split second before the car hit the tree? The glass shattered as the hood buckled, crushing against the tree trunk. Rachel reached out for him, but their fingers barely touched as the bag opened on Henry's side and he was jolted away from her.

From the back seat, Henry wanted to close his eyes, but it was like they were pinned open. He couldn't look away from her as she snapped forward. The force of the impact ripped the seatbelt and her head hit the windshield. The scream was agonizing and it took him a brief second to realize that he was screaming with his wife.

"Mr. Docking, wake up." A hand shook him awake, and Henry jumped. One of the nurses looked down at him, a kindly face hidden behind large glasses. "What were you dreaming about?"

Henry rubbed a hand over his face, touching the stubble that would grow into a full beard if he didn't do something about it soon. "The accident," he admitted.

She nodded, "Well that would explain the screaming. Maybe you should leave the hospital, just for a few hours. Get some fresh air."

He was already shaking his head before she'd even finished her sentence. "I'm fine."

She raised an eyebrow, obviously not believing him.

"Okay," he allowed, "I'm not fine but I promise I'll keep the screaming nightmares down to a minimum." He smiled to show that he was joking, but she only shook her head.

Then he heard the beeping of Rachel's machine speed up. He jumped to his feet, heart pounding. The nurse unclipped a tiny light that was attached to her belt, and checked her pupils. Rachel's hand shot up and knocked the light away from her eyes. The move was so unexpected that for a second Henry didn't know what to do.

"Mrs. Docking, can you hear me?" The nurse leaned in, examining the patient.

"What?" His wife's voice croaked with lack of use.

"What's the last thing you remember Mrs. Docking?"

Henry still couldn't move. He wanted to pinch himself, worried that he was still dreaming.

"Why do you keep calling me that?" Rachel asked, her voice rough and confused. "My last name is Sanderson. Rachel Sanderson."

Henry finally stepped forward. "Rach?"

The nurse stood upright, shaking her head. "I'm going to get a doctor."

His wife's beautiful blue eyes were tinged with a shade of red. She turned her head and looked up at him. She looked tired, sore and a little bewildered.

"I'm sorry, do I know you?"

Damn, Rachel thought, why does my whole body hurt so much? She wanted to sit up but she felt tied down by wires attached to machines. At first, she thought that the man standing over her was a doctor, but there were shadows under his eyes, a tiredness that showed that he hadn't been sleeping very well. She wondered why she felt a pang of something, like her heart ached and she had no idea why. She didn't know who he was, but when she asked if she knew him, he looked incredibly sad. He scanned her face worriedly as doctors and nurses ran tests. She felt a heavy weight on her left hand. Looking down, she saw that he held on with a tightness that might bruise.

"Rachel, can you look into the light please?"

She followed the doctor's instructions. Part of her wanted to let the stranger's hand go, but a part she didn't understand couldn't let go. If she had been in an accident maybe the man had saved her life. There was something intensely familiar about him, like he had a face that she'd seen walking through a crowd. The harsh light made her wince in discomfort. Her whole body felt sore, as if she'd been hit by a car and then reversed over for good measure.

"What happened to me?"

The doctor picked up the free hand, feeling for her pulse. "You were in an accident."

No, really, she thought sarcastically, I

never would have guessed. The other man smiled as he squeezed her hand. Besides the worry that she could see in his eyes and the tiredness casting purple shadows under them, he looked happy. Was he happy that she was awake and safe?

She couldn't shake that sense of familiarity that she felt with him, but she did her best to ignore it. Obviously she'd just been in a terrible accident and wondering about the tall, dark and good-looking man definitely wasn't high on her list of things to worry about. She didn't pull her hand out of his, but she focused on the man in the white coat. Some things weren't making a whole lot of sense, but even in the state that she was in, she could recognize a doctor.

"What is the last thing you remember?"

"I remember sitting in math class."

The doctor looked at the man standing next to her.

"But that was ten years ago," the man said. There it was again, that flash of fear and Rachel felt it, too. Something was terribly wrong.

The doctor took a deep breath and sat on the edge of her bed. "Rachel, you were in a car accident. You've been in a coma for quite some time."

If this was a joke, it really wasn't funny. At first she wanted to believe that they were lying, though deep down she knew that they had no reason to. Suddenly, she wanted to cry and she bit her bottom lip, trying to will the tears not to fall. She was in a room full of people she didn't know, and she didn't want to fall apart in front of them.

The mysterious man still stood beside her. "What can we do to get her memory back?"

"I want to keep her in for a few days, run some tests, but she should go home with you. The sooner she gets back into her routine, the better. Doing regular things will hopefully kick start the memories that she lost. We'll give you some time alone and then we'll take her upstairs."

Go home with somebody she didn't know? She briefly wondered if the doctor was joking. She watched as the nurses and doctor left and looked up at the man who'd slumped back in his chair. She wondered how long he'd been sitting there, watching over her like some guardian angel. He was someone who needed a shave in the worse possible way, but still an angel.

Rachel took a deep breath and looked around the hospital room. She knew that she was avoiding the issue, but it was hard enough getting her own head around the memory loss. "What's your name?" she finally asked.

It might not have been the ideal first question, but it would have to do. The man looked shocked. He already knew about the memory loss, but it looked like he was having a hard time dealing with it himself.

"It's Henry." His voice was gruff and slightly hoarse, like it hadn't been used for a while.

Though she already suspected the answer, she had to ask the next question brewing in her mind. There was a part of her that she hoped was wrong, and the other hoped that she was right. She wondered if it was the old and new parts of her personality at war with each other. She looked down at her hands; the knuckles were white as she gripped the bed sheet tightly.

"Do I know you?"

Henry nodded and looked down at the floor.

"And how do I know you?"

"We're married. We've been married for a while."

Married? But that was impossible, how could she be married when she was only twenty-five? Henry must have noticed the bewildered look on her face, and his guarded expression became softer. "Rachel, you lost ten years."

A few days later, for the first time since the accident, Henry left his wife and went home. He collected everything about their life together, the wedding pictures and photographs from when they'd gone on vacation, and he hid them. The doctor had warned him that too much visual information could ruin the chance of Rachel getting her memory back forever. He was supposed to show her this at regular intervals, maybe even weeks apart.

It had been a small wedding, just them and two witnesses. She wore a simple white sleeveless dress, and her hair had been pinned up. She'd looked absolutely beautiful.

It was going to kill him but he had to be strong. If he tried to force her into getting her memory back, it wouldn't do them any good and could even make things worse. When he was finally done, he got back into the car. It was time to meet his wife.

Nervous really didn't cover it. Rachel packed up her things into the small suitcase, sat on her hospital bed and waited for the man who was her husband. This felt strange to her. He was her rock, the only thing tying her to her old life. The day he told her that she was an orphan, that they both were, and that it was one of the things that drew them together had been one of the hardest days of her life.

Henry seemed nice, though she was still getting her head around the fact she was married to him. The next few weeks were going to be strange. The doctors said that if she was ever going to get her memory back it would within those weeks. She might start remembering bits and pieces, but it was going to take a lot longer for her to remember everything.

"How are you feeling?"

Rachel looked up and into the eyes of her husband. There was that feeling again, the feeling that she knew him, like a face in the crowd.

"I'm okay. How are you?"

Henry smiled. "I'm okay. I brought the car, so we can go home."

There was an awkward silence. She really hoped that it wouldn't always be like this. They were married, so they had to have something in common.

The first few days were terrible. They barely talked to each other. Rachel had the master bedroom and Henry slept on the settee. It was on the fourth day that Henry showed her their wedding pictures. She had woken up to the smell of coffee and walked downstairs for a cup. The first thing she saw was Henry standing with his back to her. He wore a pair of black jogging pants and nothing else.

Her heart skipped a beat. He was a good looking man and obviously kept himself in a good shape. It felt right to go to him, plant a kiss on his back, and hug him. The fact it felt right wasn't what stopped her. It was like her body remembered everything, the way that it was reacting to the sight of him. It was only her brain that stopped her from going to him.

"I made it just the way you like it."

Memory flooded through her mind.

She'd gotten up late that day. He'd made her breakfast and since she wasn't in a rush, she'd gone downstairs naked. She'd never been too worried about walking around naked. Some woman might be self-conscious, but she knew that her husband loved every inch of her. When she'd walked into the kitchen Henry had been reading the morning paper at the kitchen table. The idea had come to her quickly.

He barely looked up as she walked in, but she could see the smile that spread across his face. She confidently walked up and straddled him. Lowering the newspaper that separated them, she winked at him.

"If this is the reward I get for making you breakfast, I'll start doing it more often." He threw the paper onto the floor and stole her lips with his. The way he barely touched her breasts made the nipples rock hard.

She could already feel his rock hard cock barely contained by his jogging pants. It wouldn't the first time they had sex on the kitchen table, but it would be the first time food hadn't been involved. He gently pushed her back onto the table until she was lying down. She raised her legs and he buried his head between them. She'd always loved the feel of his tongue as it teased her clit. As he licked and flicked with his tongue, he started to work his fingers in and out of her wet pussy. The warm heat of the sun came in through the window, and she was suddenly thankful the kitchen faced the garden so no neighbors would be able to see anything.

The first orgasm hit her out of nowhere. One second she was enjoying her husband pleasuring her, and then her pussy gushed with hot liquid.

She moaned with pleasure as she ground her pussy against his tongue and lips. He spread her legs apart, pulled down his jogging pants, and in one thrust, he buried himself into her wet pussy. He played with her breasts as he fucked her. She always drove him to distraction. She knew the effect she had on him. They'd had sex in so many places in the house, there wasn't a room they hadn't marked with moans, sweat and sex. She pushed him off of her and then turned herself around so her belly rested on the table.

"What do you want, my love?" he asked, taut with desire.

"I want you to grab my hair and fuck my ass."

He moaned at her words. He played with her ass, spreading the wetness between her legs to the tight hole between her ass cheeks. It felt so decadent, so taboo, and she loved every minute of it. It was when he pushed one finger into her impossibly tight hole and played with her clit that she came so hard she worried that his hold might slip. He pushed another finger into her and when he removed them, she cried out in protest.

Then he rubbed his cock against her dark hole. She moaned and could only mumble inarticulately; it was only the need that was driving her. He inched it in slowly, making sure that his cock was wet with her juices. She didn't mind a little pain, but there was a fine line between that and pleasure. She gripped onto the table, her clit pushing against the hard wood, and she knew that every time he pushed into her, it would rub against the table. It was going to be a delicious combination of pleasure.

"Rachel? Are you okay?" Henry's voice broke into her flashback.

Her face felt incredibly hot. Had that really happened or was it a fantasy? She looked at her feet, and tried to will the blush away.

Suddenly Henry stood in front of her and his fingertips touched her chin, lifting her face, and he looked into her eyes. "Did you remember something?"

The possible flashback and having him standing so close was as distracting as hell. The blush was back in full force.

"I don't know." She looked at the kitchen table, "Have we ever, you know, had sex on the table?"

The laugh that came out of him was startling and so manly that it nearly made her knees go weak. "We've done it a lot. It's strange that out of all our memories together, that's the one you remember."

"It was you, seeing you half naked making coffee. It reminded me." Rachel stepped out of his reach and picked up the coffee. "Can you tell me about the accident?"

Henry had been dreading this moment. He was glad it looked like they were finally getting back on track and she was slowly starting to remember things. He'd just hoped that he would have more time, that she would want to remember the good memories first.

"I want to have kids Henry. I don't know why you're being so difficult about this."

It wasn't the first time they'd had this conversation. They'd been together for ten years and she'd made no secret about the fact she wanted kids. Henry, on the other hand, had never wanted kids. Except for this, though, he thought it was incredible that he'd met a woman who completed him and matched him on every level.

"I'm going to be thirty-five next year. I don't want to wait much longer."

"Why do you want kids?"

"Why don't you want kids?" she countered quickly.

"Life's pretty much perfect as we are. Kids would complicate things."

Rachel walked to the kitchen and Henry followed her. He watched as she downed her glass of wine. They were supposed to be going out tonight. Everything had been perfect but then she had to bring this up.

"Henry you're just selfish. You don't want to share me with anyone. Look, we've got to go, Hailey is expecting us." She readjusted her earrings and slipped her shoes on. It surprised him how quickly they'd started arguing.

It seemed like a lifetime ago that they'd been naked in each other's arms. They had showered together an hour ago and she'd gotten down on her knees and sucked him off. When she got back onto her feet and kissed him, it was sexy tasting himself on her lips. He wondered if she felt the same when he went down on her. Where had the gentle comfort of the afternoon vanished to?

That night, the air was thick with tension. They might not have argued often, but when they did it was pretty intense. They should have resolved the argument before they got in the car but they hadn't.

Rachel put the cup of coffee down. "So we had an argument about kids and that's why we crashed?"

"No, we crashed because of the rabbit that thought that standing in the middle of the road was a good idea. I just can't help blaming myself for the accident. Maybe if we hadn't argued about having kids, then I wouldn't have swerved without crashing."

"That's stupid," she scoffed.

Henry frowned. "Excuse me?"

"It could have been a lot worse. We could have died in that accident, Henry. Sure, I didn't come out of it completely unscathed but at least my memories are coming back."

"And what about the kids?" he asked hesitantly.

"It's an argument that I don't even remember having, and when I do, we'll talk about it again. I don't remember most of the last ten years we spent together so I can't really be angry with you about an argument that I've forgotten."

Henry couldn't help but smile. "When you're ready, when you can remember everything, I just want you to know that I'm ready for kids now."

She looked a little taken aback. "You are?"

"It took almost losing you to realize that I want kids with you."

She kept having flashbacks. She would walk into a room and remember something. It was mostly sexual — they'd had a lot of sex in this house. The only things that she couldn't remember were happier times, ones that didn't just involve sex.

They still slept in separate rooms, but they'd started to eat together and watch TV. These were nice moments and she was starting to feel a lot more comfortable with her husband. It was at the end of the next week that Henry suggested doing something completely different.

"You want to go on a date?" Henry smiled at her. "I thought it would be nice to go to the place we went on a first date."

"Where's that?"

Henry reached into his pocket and pulled out a blindfold. He walked hesitantly towards her, as if he was nervous and she felt it as well. "It's a surprise."

He was startled that she actually let him blindfold her. They sat in the car in silence. He opened a window and watched as she turned her head slightly, catching the cool wind on her face. He'd noticed that she was remembering more and more things, but she wasn't telling him what they were. By the red blush that seemed to constantly be on her face these days, it was obvious that she was remembering the sex they used to have.

It felt strange that in the two weeks that

she'd been back at home they hadn't had sex. It had been the longest time that they'd gone without it. It felt nice to connect on a different level.

He wondered if she'd remember the last time they'd used a blindfold, and if the thought made her wet, because it made him hard. He took a deep breath as he readjusted his jeans and focused on driving.

"So where are you taking me?"

He smiled. "I said it's a surprise."

She liked the sound of his voice. He turned on the music and filled the silence with old school rock music. He sang along to it under his breath. The tune was familiar, maybe it was one of her favorites.

Rachel enjoyed being blindfolded a little too much. She liked letting Henry take control and she briefly wondered if they'd done something like this before. She was starting to feel a little turned on, a mixed bag of anticipation and nerves. She had no idea where he was taking her, but she put herself in his hands.

Suddenly the car stopped and Henry got out She was tempted to remove the blindfold but kept her hands in her laps. Her door opened and she looked up, smiling. "Can I take the blindfold off?"

She could sense the hesitation. Why was he worried? Maybe it was something to do with the date. Maybe he was worried that she wouldn't remember anything about this place. Henry took one of her hands and helped her out of the car.

"Keep it on for a little longer."

Her shoes crunched as they touched the gravel pathway. She could hear voices. Some belonged to children, which meant that whereever they were, there were families.

This was getting stranger and stranger. They walked a short distance and suddenly she could smell flowers. The smell was a little overpowering and tickled her nose. The sneeze took her completely by surprise and it made Henry laugh.

"Okay, time to take the blindfold off."

He stood behind her and removed it. The first thing she saw was the flowers. There had to be thousands of them. They were all different colors, and nestled in their soft surface lay a blanket set out with wine, food and a stereo.

She remembered this. It wasn't like a flood of memories but something clicked in her head about the two of them in this garden. They'd met the week before in a bookshop when they'd ended up reaching for the same book. Their hands touched, he'd made a joke, and they had laughed.

It was here in the garden that they'd kissed for the first time, surprisingly chaste and sweet. It had fired up all kinds of passion, but it hadn't been until their third date that they had sex.

Henry was looking at her with questions and hope in his eyes. That was the thing with Henry: she could always read what he was feeling in his eyes. "Rach, are you alright?"

She smiled. "I'm feeling a lot better." She stepped towards him, raised up onto her toes and brushed her lips against his. She could feel his uncertainty as he kissed her back.

He pulled away and looked down at her. "What do you remember?"

"That I love you. I won't lie to you, there are few things that I don't remember. Okay, probably more than a few things. All I remember now is this, our first date. The fact you were so nervous, you accidentally spilled wine down my top. I remember our first kiss. We just needed to keep working at it, Henry. It's going to come back, all of it, eventually."

4 FALLING BACK IN LOVE

Victor opened the letter. He'd known that it would arrive eventually. He hadn't seen his wife for nearly two years. Their last argument had been huge. She'd left and Victor had let her go. He knew that in the long run he wouldn't have been able to stop her. Forcing her to stay would have made it worse.

He pulled a thin stack of paper from the envelope. He paced in his office as he flipped through the papers. He couldn't help the anger that seemed to grow like a beast in his stomach. She wanted a divorce, and she hadn't even come to deliver the papers by hand. He felt so angry, not just at her, but at his own weakness.

It felt like a lifetime ago when they'd

first met. It had been a whirlwind romance. He'd been in Malibu on business, and she'd been giving a lecture at one of the local high schools about art. He said if he'd had her as a teacher, then maybe he would have done better in art. She'd rolled her eyes at the obvious pick up line. Her long brunette hair had been braided over her shoulder, and a short fringe skimmed across her forehead, bringing his attention to vibrant green eyes.

Then, she asked him out to dinner.

Her forwardness had taken him completely by surprise. He'd originally thought that she was shy, but her flirtatious look was completely at odds with her appearance.

The relationship had started out as being purely physical. They hadn't lived in the same city, but whenever Victor was in Malibu, he went to see her. The sex had been incredible; the best he'd ever had. Then, eventually, sex had turned into a relationship. It had been an odd way to go about it but it had worked for them.

One day, they started to argue. It never started with anything big, but it always ended the same: sex, and they had it down to a fine art. Victor had started to think that maybe it was the reason they started arguing. But then it went too far. He never hit her, but he pushed her one night and she'd fallen. She hadn't been hurt but she'd left.

And he'd never seen her again.

He sat down and started to look through the papers, swallowing the anger. He scrolled through the pages, looking for the reason. She hadn't written about the arguments.

It had been two years, but he still missed her. It didn't surprise him that he didn't want to sign the papers. Even though he'd known this day was coming, it still hurt him. He knew that she was still in Malibu, probably living with her mother. He'd always known where she was, but he'd never gone after her.

Maybe he should have, at least to say sorry for his behavior. He wondered if she ever thought of him or if she viewed him as a mistake she'd be glad to get rid of. He closed the pages and slipped the unsigned document back into the envelope.

He picked up the phone and called his secretary, asking her to buy plane tickets for later today. She mentioned a few meetings that she needed to cancel, but nothing was too important to miss. If anything critical came up, he could always get his brother Frank to cover it.

He had somewhere important to go.

It was a beautiful day. Juliet looked out of the window of her mother's house. It usually wasn't this quiet, but her mother was out shopping with Cullum. Juliet liked the privacy. From this room, she had a spectacular view of the beach, and the way the sunlight bounced off the sea made it look like it was a sheet of glass. This was the room she did the majority of her painting in, and canvases were lined up against the wall. A few of her paintings were up around the house; she had them all on rotation. It just seemed fair. Well, as fair as anything can be involving paintings.

The doorbell rang loudly through the house. It made her jump. She had always hated it, but she hadn't been able to talk her mother into changing it. Jobs teaching art were few and far between. She was lucky to have the temp job at Rahul High, but it was only because the current teacher had just given birth and was on leave. Returning home had been a welcome change from New York City. She found the city cold and windy and the people unfriendly. Traveling in a taxi had always been unpleasant, but the swear words those taxi drivers used had been educational as well.

She could see a shadow through the frosted glass of the front door. Probably a salesman, she thought. It was tempting to just ignore it, but her mom had brought her up with manners. She opened the door, and the smile froze on her face.

He hadn't changed much. The only thing different was the lack of a suit. She remembered a time when they'd made a joke about how he didn't own a pair of jeans. It was always like he was ready to go to the office. Seeing him made her stomach twist. It wasn't an unpleasant feeling but there was an edge of panic that she couldn't shake. She stepped out, closing the door behind her.

"Victor," she said calmly. "What are you doing here?"

He had that look on his face, the one that told her that he liked what he saw. He had a backpack over his shoulder and the casual clothes he wore made him look a lot younger. His dark hair had grown out from the business cut he'd had before.

"Hey Juliet, can I come in?"

"No." If he came in, he'd see the kid's toys and then the questions would start, questions that Juliet didn't know how to answer. She took a deep breath. "Now isn't a good time."

She thought back to when her mother had left with Cullum. How long did she have until they came back? Not long.

"I got the divorce papers."

"So you came to deliver them in person?" she asked skeptically. The Victor she'd known had left personal things like gifts to be delivered by his staff. Sometimes he'd been so cold she wondered how they'd managed to get married.

"Actually, I wanted to talk." He reached into his back pocket and pulled out a card. "I'm staying at this hotel, and I'll be in Malibu until the end of next week. I'll sign the papers, but I want to talk first. Can you meet me tomorrow?"

This was a bad idea, but it was still better than talking at home. "I can't make it in the afternoon, but I'm free in the evening." Thankfully her mom didn't have anything to do and she'd look after Cullum.

"Okay, I'll meet you in the bar."

"Okay."

He smiled. "It's good to see you, Jules."

Victor unpacked his bag. There was a time he would have paid extra for room service to do it for him. These days, he didn't bother. He was a grown man, and he could look after himself, or at least he could start.

Seeing Juliet had completely blown him away. She looked so relaxed and happy. He remembered the almost physical change that happened just after they moved back to New York. It was like the big city had sucked the life out of her. He knew that seeing him would startle her, and he was lucky that she didn't close the door in his face.

At least tomorrow they'd be able to talk. He could apologize and get that much needed closure that he was desperate for.

"Who are you meeting?" her mother asked.

"Just a friend. It shouldn't take long, but tonight was the only night I could meet him before he left again." Juliet added a flick of mascara and liner.

She knew why she was putting this much effort into seeing him. She didn't want him to think she was struggling. Life wasn't great at the moment, and while she loved her mom for letting them stay with her, it was still odd. He obviously knew she was living with her mom, that was the only reason he'd found her so easily, but tonight was going to involve some creative truth telling.

"You're meeting a man?" Juliet could hear that her mom was smiling. She'd been pushing Juliet to start dating again. Although Juliet had said goodbye to Victor in her heart, the space that had been left had been promptly filled by Cullum. Would she be able to get rid of Victor before he found out about his son? What would happen if he found out? Would he try to get custody of him? Victor was a powerful man, and she was sure that he'd get whatever he wanted.

She undid her hair and brushed a comb through it before she stood up and checked out her reflection in the mirror. It was a simple black dress. Every woman had one in their wardrobe and this was Juliet's. The cut was flattering; she had a few curves but this dress kicked off from the hip, adding a beautiful flowing effect. She slipped on her red heels, ran her fingers through her hair and smiled at her reflection. "What gave me away?"

"Well, you usually don't look this sexy when you're just meeting friends."

She smiled at her mom. "It isn't important. I should be back in a few hours."

"Take your time, Cullum's been quiet today so we'll watch movies and I'll put him to bed at seven." The older woman winked at her. "Have a good night out."

Juliet shook her head in disbelief. Would her mother be that happy for her to get out if she knew that she was meeting with Cullum's dad? She'd never really told her mother what had happened. She hadn't even known she was pregnant until a week or two after shc'd moved in with her mom. In hindsight she knew that leaving had been the best decision. He hadn't meant to hurt her; it was an argument that just got out of hand. Before she'd found out that she was pregnant she thought that she might go back to him. They'd needed to talk and work on their marriage, but then she found out she was pregnant. There never seemed to be a good time to call Victor. Days had turned into months and Cullum was born.

There was no way she could tell him now. He'd looked so relaxed when he'd knocked on her door, and she wondered if he had changed. How would he react if he found out that she had their child and never told him? Not well, probably.

"I'm just going to give Cullum a kiss, if you need me, just call."

"Everything will be fine. Have fun Juliet."

Victor was nervous. He tapped his

fingers against the bar top. Anyone would think that he was on a date, not about to meet his wife to discuss their divorce. He fiddled with his shirt. He'd been tempted to wear one of his suits but decided against it. Juliet might have found it intimating to face him in a suit and to him it felt like armor. He'd ended up wearing a blue and white checked shirt with short sleeves that revealed toned and tanned arms. The jeans were dark blue and he completed the outfit with a pair of polished black shoes. He looked good, but he would have been more comfortable in a suit.

He took a drink from his beer, this time tapping his fingers against the cool bottle. He looked up at the mirror that was just behind the bar and stopped tapping his fingers. At first he didn't recognize her. She looked completely different from the woman who'd worn long skirts and halter tops.

The dress was simple but clung to all the right places. He remembered one of their dates; they'd flirted all night, pretending that it was their first date night. The way she'd brushed against him had made him rock hard. He'd whispered in her ear that he wanted to fuck her so bad and he loved the way she'd blushed. They barely got out of the bar, when she'd dragged him into the nearest alleyway and let him feel that she wasn't wearing any underwear. As he fucked her fast and hard against the wall, she'd bitten his shoulder to muffle the sound of her moans.

It had been so hot and the memory made him hard again as he watched her walk towards the bar. He wondered if her skin still felt as soft as it looked. She smiled at him, and he had to wonder if she knew the effect she was having on him.

"I bought you a drink," he offered. "Do you still like martinis?"

He watched as she brought the drink to her lips, and the tip of her tongue flicked out a second before she took a sip. "Thanks."

"Damn, you look good." The words slipped out before he could stop them. There was the barest hint of a blush before she tipped her head forward, her hair masking her face.

"What did you want to talk about, Victor? It's been two years and I haven't heard from you. Why now?"

He took a deep drink. "I know that you're set on this divorce and I'll send the papers, but I wanted to tell you something first."

"Tell me what?"

"That I'm sorry. I'm sorry I scared you. I'm sorry that I never came after you. I'm sorry that I never realized how unhappy you were." He still couldn't see her face, couldn't see what reaction his words were having on her. Did she care? Did she believe him? "Did you want to get something to eat? We could talk properly."

She flicked her hair over her shoulder and he could read the uncertainty in her gray eyes. "Okay, but it's just dinner, Victor. Thank you for apologizing, but it doesn't change anything."

He quickly got them a table. He usually liked taking charge, but this whole encounter was throwing him off balance. She took a brief look at the menu and told the waitress to bring two steaks. That surprised him and he couldn't keep the look off his face.

"Well," she said, smiling, "you are paying, aren't you?"

"Of course. Are you still planning on ordering dessert?"

"See, you do still know me."

She was enjoying this way too much. It felt like a step into the past. She let go of the fear she had been holding onto. He'd never find out about his son. Whatever happened was just too unpredictable and if she could get away with waiting until Cullum was old enough to make his own decisions then she would. For now she would enjoy this moment, because that was all they were going to have: this moment.

They talked about the past. They talked about everything besides Cullum or the divorce. It felt like a first date and it was nice. The way that he looked at her made her feel beautiful. They finished the meal and she wondered how far she could push it.

She reached out with her foot; the table was small so it didn't take much of a stretch to touch his leg with her bare foot. She wasn't worried about anyone watching, the table cloth came all the way to the floor.

His dark eyes widened in surprise. "What are you doing?"

She trailed her foot up his leg. He spread them slightly, giving her easier access and she rested her foot on the chair. She flexed her toes slightly, brushing the growing bulge between her soon-to-be ex-husband's legs.

"I'm thinking of ways that we can say goodbye." She massaged his cock with her foot.

She watched as he swallowed, hard. "What did you have in mind?"

She played with the rim of the glass as she rolled her foot. "You've got a room upstairs?" She smiled as he bit back a groan.

"Are you sure that you want to do this?"

"I'm going to go upstairs to collect the papers anyway. We might as well entertain ourselves, and as I remember, we used to be pretty good at it. That is, of course unless you don't want to." Juliet curled her foot slightly and cupped the outline of his hard cock.

Victor groaned again, this time a little louder, drawing the attention of the older couple not sitting that far away. Juliet smiled politely at the woman. "He had the vanilla cheesecake, it was divine. You should try it."

The older woman looked bemused. "Thank you, dear."

She was amazing. Victor had never been turned on so much by a woman. It was funny that it was his soon-to-be ex-wife that was torturing with the delicate movements of her foot. He was suddenly thankful that he'd worn jeans. The tight fabric held his raging hard-on under control. With a quick movement of his hand, he adjusted his shirt to cover it.

This was all she wanted from him. He thought that the relationship could be saved, but it was clear that she wasn't even going to entertain the idea. He wasn't going to push it; as soon as he did, he knew that she'd pull away.

They barely got to the thankfully empty elevator before she pushed him against the wall and started to assault his lips with hot passion. He pulled up her dress, feeling the tender flesh just above the stockings that she was wearing. He groaned as he realized that she was wearing a thong. She hooked her leg around his hip and started to rub herself against him. He was so hard that he thought that he might explode before he even got inside of her.

He reached down, gently touching the wet patch that was starting to spread across her panties. He pulled her thong aside and slowly inserted a finger. Her wet, slick muscles gripped onto his finger and he worked it in and out. He loved the way she groaned. He rubbed his thumb against her clit and she came with a shudder.

"I love how you look when you come. You're so damn beautiful."

He ran his free hand through her hair, pushing it away from her face, and kissed her again. The elevator stopped and he looked at the number. They'd hit the penthouse and he retrieved his card, the only way to enter his rooms.

"Why am I not surprised that you have

the penthouse suite?"

"Because you know I like the best."

He headed to the kitchen, getting two glasses and pouring out a healthy amount of whiskey in each. He couldn't wait to make love to her but he needed to get rid of his hard on. He was pretty sure that he wouldn't have this chance again. He wanted to worship her body; he wanted to feel her come around his hard cock. She was already wet, so aroused that he was sure that the top of her thighs were wet with juices. He handed her one of the glasses. Her pupils were so dark that it seemed to drown out all the color of her irises.

Victor watched as she put the glass down, lifted the skirt of her dress and pulled it over her head. Everything matched: the black lace of the thong and the black fabric of the push up bra cupping her white breasts. The stockings were attached to a garter belt that covered her hips. She was beautiful, and his cock twitched to life. She picked up the glass again, resting it against her hip. She left her bag on the kitchen table.

"Not interested in foreplay?"

"We had foreplay in the elevator. Where's the bedroom?"

She might not have planned on sleeping with him, but she'd obviously made the right choice in underwear judging by the look on his face. She was so wet from the elevator. He remembered exactly how to touch her. She'd never come so hard, but it didn't surprise her. It had been two years since she'd last had sex. The intensity of him fingering her in the elevator had left her speechless.

Her skin felt feverish and she rolled the cool edge of her glass across her skin. The bedroom was large, the bed still made. The duvet was a rich shade of crimson and as she put the glass down, she ran her hand over the soft fabric.

Victor entered behind her, and she turned around. It was like the last two years had never happened and for one night she wanted to forget them. She wanted to be with the man who drove her insane with desire, who knew every curve of her body and would make her body sweat and shudder with pleasure.

She didn't bother to kick off the heels; she would need the extra height. Juliet went to him and as he reached down to release his raging hard on, she stopped him. He raised an eyebrow in question but she brushed a kiss across his lips.

"Let me," she whispered.

She quickly undid his jeans and as she pulled them down, she dropped to her knees. Juliet reached up and pulled down his boxers, allowing his cock to stand straight and hard. She flicked her hair back over her shoulder, not wanting him to miss anything that she was about to do. Gazing up at him, she held his hard shaft with one hand and licked the head. Victor's hands went into her hair and he guided her with a slight pressure on the back of her head. She moved slowly and deliberately. If she wanted him to come inside of her wet pussy, she had to make sure that she didn't push him too far.

It didn't take long before Victor tugged on her hair and she released the gentle suction that she'd created around his cock.

"You're so good at that." He reached down and picked her up. She wrapped her legs around his waist. His cock pushed at her wet hole as he carried her to the bed and half lowered, half dropped her. She couldn't help the giggle that escaped her lips and Victor quickly swallowed it with a kiss. She groaned as he pushed into her wet folds, moving her thong to the side again. It felt so decadent and naughty, fucking her with her underwear still on.

"You feel so good inside me," she whispered against his ear and he groaned in response. "Fuck me Victor, fuck me hard."

Victor pulled away, though his cock was

still heavy inside of her. "I'm not just going to fuck you. I'm going to make you scream my name."

She thought that he was going to pound inside of her, but he started slowly. It felt delicious; the way the friction built up was unbearable. She wrapped her legs back around his waist, wanting to feel him deeper inside of her.

His hands traveled over her breasts and pulled the fabric down so he could touch her nipples. They were so hard and sensitive to the touch. She moaned under his tender ministrations. He took one of her nipples into his mouth, flicking at the hard nub and she came, the pleasure catching her up in its wave, until she came crashing down.

She felt Victor's hands on her hips and he started to build up the delicious speed. Juliet pulled him down and kissed him. His name escaped her lips and she caught his smile. He started to pound into her harder; suddenly she was coming in waves again and as her wet pussy tightly gripped onto his hard cock, he groaned and she could feel it pulsate and release. She was suddenly thankful that he'd remembered the condom.

Victor slumped on top of Juliet. "Were we always so good at that?" He liked the way that she giggled underneath him.

"I think we got it down to a fine art."

"Is that your phone?"

Suddenly Juliet was pushing him off. She darted back to the kitchen and Victor followed her. She opened her bag and retrieved her phone.

"Mom? What's wrong?" She turned her back to Victor and he could see her shoulders become tense. "Where are you? Is he okay?"

Victor collected his jeans and cleaned himself up as Juliet talked on the phone. There was an audible click as she closed her phone and retrieved her dress. "What's wrong?" he asked.

"I have to get to the hospital. It's an emergency. I need to call a taxi."

"Don't be silly Juliet. I rented a car, I can take you."

Juliet bit her lip. "Okay, but I have to tell you something in the car."

Damn it all to hell. Juliet thought she could get away without telling Victor, but she couldn't do that now. Being with him had stirred up old feelings. They rode in the car in silence as she tried to sort through her emotions. She'd never stopped loving Victor, but she thought that they were too different. He loved New York, while she hated it with a violent passion. She used the accident as an excuse to leave.

"Who's in the hospital?"

She took a deep breath. "Cullum."

Victor took a deep breath. "Who is he," he asked carefully. "A boyfriend?"

Juliet looked out the window. "No, he isn't a boyfriend." Maybe we shouldn't be having this conversation in a moving vehicle, she thought.

"Come on Juliet, you're killing me here."

"He's my son." She could only barely whisper the words. The car swerved slightly before Victor got himself under control. They drove the rest of the way in silence as Juliet let him process the news. All she could think about was her son. Her mom had said that he'd been feeling unwell all day, that was probably why he'd been so quiet. Then he'd started running a fever, so her mom had brought him to the hospital. Juliet felt terrible, she should have been home, and she shouldn't have been reliving the past.

Victor parked the car and Juliet rushed out, not bothering to see if he was following her. She got to the front desk and told the nurse Cullum's name. It seemed to take forever for the woman to check on the computer for her son.

"Just follow the red line on the floor. It will take you to the waiting room."

When she got there, another nurse was

talking to her mom. "How is he? Where is he?"

"Sweetheart, he's fine. The nurse just told me that they're going to keep him in for observation and to give him some fluids. He's asleep for now. I'm going to head home and get him some clean clothes for tomorrow. You can go sit in with him. I'll see you soon."

A minute later, Juliet was sitting next to her son's bed. Her mom had been right, he was fast asleep and she reached out, picking up his hand. He was beautiful, a perfect blend of his mom and dad. He had her gray eyes and Victor's dark hair. If she hadn't been so preoccupied about Victor then she would have noticed he was sick earlier. She ran a hand over her eyes and realized that she was crying.

"This isn't your fault." Victor put his hand on her shoulder; he could tell that she was crying. "I always knew that you would make a terrific mother and I was right."

"You wouldn't say that if you knew the truth."

"Are you honestly telling me that you intentionally gave your son a bug? I find that hard to believe." He saw her hand tighten on Cullum's. "Look, he'll be all right."

"Do you know that he's your son?"

The words came out of nowhere, but they didn't surprise him. He'd always know about Cullum, though he hadn't known his son's name. He thought that when she was ready she'd tell him or not. She hadn't trusted him and he'd wanted to give her space. His heart melted when he looked down at the sleeping child.

"I know."

Juliet looked up, surprise evident on her face. "How long have you known?"

"Your mom told me. I've been giving her money to put into an account for him. I thought that I lost you and I wanted to wait until you were ready. Then, when I got the papers, I had to see you. I wanted to apologize. Then tonight happened and I finally got to meet him. I wish it was under better circumstances. If you want me to leave I will. I'll sign the papers but I had to see him, both of you." Victor held his breath.

"Stay," Juliet said with a small smile. "Please."

5 SUBMITTING TO THE MAN UPSTAIRS

I carried the last box up to the apartment. It was heavy work and since I was doing it in the middle of the afternoon, the apartment block was pretty much empty of residents. This taught me for buying a flat near the top of a seven story building with no working elevator, I berated myself as I climbed the stairs. Oh no, I wanted privacy, I wanted a nice quiet room to do my work as a freelance writer. Unfortunately I didn't have the money or the resources to move to a cottage in the country. The small flat was just going to have to do.

I balanced the box, which contained some food and a bottle of Coke, which I was dying to take a deep drink from. I dug deep into my jeans pocket, wrestled for my new front door key and pulled it free. I could hear footsteps from the stairs heading down from the top floor. Curiosity got the better of me and I waited until I could see one of my new neighbors. Using my foot I made sure that the front door wouldn't close on me and waited.

The first person I saw was the blonde, so beautiful that she could have been on the front cover of the magazines I never bothered to read. It was the man who stood just behind her, following her down the stairs, that made my jaw hang open. To say he was unbelievably sexy would be an understatement. He was so beautiful that he made my body ache. The fact he was topless, showing off a well-defined chest, made it hard for me to drag my eyes away. He must have sensed my eyes on him because he turned just before they vanished from view and winked at me.

My cheeks went hot and I quickly ducked through my door. I guessed that tall, dark and handsome was my upstairs neighbor, unless of course the blond was kicking out the shirtless man in the middle of the afternoon but I pretty much doubted it. I certainly wouldn't kick that guy out of bed.

While it might be a great way to waste some time thinking of him, I needed to get the computer set up. Being freelance meant I needed to get online as soon as possible, or I wouldn't be writing or submitting any stories. This really wasn't an option.

I'd finally finished setting up the computer when I heard someone knocking on the door. The only one who knew I'd moved in yet was Mister Half-Naked. I ran a hand through my curly black locks, took a deep breath and opened the front door. I tried really hard to hide my disappointment when I saw an elderly woman on my doorstep. I smiled when I saw the tray that she was holding.

"Hello," she greeted cheerily. "I just wanted to welcome you to the building. I'm Michelle, me and my husband Donald live just below you." She handed me the tray. "I made cupcakes."

"Wow, thank you." I took them from her and peeked under the kitchen cloth she'd put over it, they were covered with pink icing. "Do you want to come in? I've managed to dig out my kettle and cups." I stepped aside.

"I would love to." She was a quaint little old lady, and I was sure that under the nice exterior she was curious about the new neighbor. I was also sure that by the end of the week everyone in the building was going to know about me and probably the layout of my flat as well.

I apologized about the mess as I made a pot of tea and joined Michelle in the living room. As soon as we were settled I asked the one big question that was preying on my mind. "Who lives above me?"

I swear that the older woman blushed. "So you've seen him then? He usually doesn't make an appearance until the afternoon."

"Who is he?"

She leaned forward, holding the cup and saucer in her small hands and smiled. The smile made her look a lot younger than she obviously was. "His name is Ian Gild and he's the most charming man that you're ever going to meet."

"He came downstairs with a girl. Does he live with anybody?" Now it was really starting to sound like a conversation I would have been having at high school.

The older woman shook her head. "He has clients."

Oh my god, he was an escort? Well he certainly was good looking enough to be one and with that lazy smile I could imagine that he left plenty of woman satisfied. The older woman must have read my expression because suddenly she was laughing. She was laughing so hard that she had to put down her cup. "I'm sorry, dear, I just figured out how that must have sounded. Ian works from home but I'm not sure who the woman might have been. He hasn't had a serious girlfriend. I've never found out why."

Maybe he was gay. The thought barely passed through my head before I instantly dismissed it. The fact he was walking a girl downstairs in an obvious state of undress kind of ruled out the gay theory and the way he'd looked at me. Like I was a dessert that he couldn't wait to try, well it would be really unfair if he ended up being gay.

We quickly finished our cups of tea and Michelle left me to get back to unpacking. Before she left she said that if I ever wanted anything all I had to do was ask. She and the husband would be happy to help.

I left the boxes unpacked. I'd been rushing around all day, I just needed a break and to check the online job board for any work. After that I was going to have a very cold shower. I'd never met a guy that had such an effect on me. We hadn't even been introduced yet.

I rarely left my apartment for the first week. I spent the majority of the time opening the unpacked boxes and writing up articles. I also started work on a few short stories. Work might have been hard but I was doing something that I loved so I really couldn't complain. Over the course of the week I had plenty of visitors, and most of them dropped off food. I had enough now that I wouldn't have to worry about leaving the flat until the middle of next week.

The only one who hadn't said hello was Ian. I was a little disappointed, after that weird moment in the hall I was sure that he would have at least introduced himself. Anyway, he was a busy boy. Unless I was listening to my music I could frequently hear his door being knocked on and then opened. After the first few times, the routine was pretty much the same.

Some girl would knock on his door. I would hear muffled conversation and half an hour down the line I could hear moaning that made me jealous and left me blushing like mad. I stuffed my ear phones in and worked. I wasn't sure if it was the same girl but whenever I saw somebody come down the stairs, they were all different. Maybe I hadn't been wrong with the escort theory.

It was in the middle of my third week in my new home when I'd finally had enough. This girl was so loud that she made my living room vibrate. It really only left me with one option. I had to go for a walk. When I finally got back, slightly wet from the rain and not in a better mood I took the stairs up to his apartment. I had no idea if he was entertaining anyone else but at this point I was beyond caring.

I banged on the door, hard. Pain shot up my arm and made it go numb. As I was doing a little dance, waving my arm around like an idiot, his front door opened. This time he was completely dressed, a bemused expression on his face as he watched me. I scowled at him, but he looked good. He looked so good in fact I was a little lost for words.

"Can I help you?" He had one hand on the door, leaning in a way that made him look a little bored. The smile was lazy; his dark eyes were hooded and unreadable.

I took a deep breath, and tried to focus on not blushing. "Actually you can. I live downstairs and I'm not sure if you know this but the walls are very thin."

He frowned. "You moved into Steve's old place?"

I nodded. Steve had been a nice old man but as deaf as a lamppost, he'd probably never heard anything that went on upstairs. If he'd known he'd probably would have died of a heart attack instead of moving to warmer weather. "I don't know what you do up here but please keep it down. I work from home and I usually like a little quiet while I work."

"What do you do?"

"I'm a writer."

His smile seemed to get wider and it confused the hell out of me. It wasn't the first response I usually got when I told somebody what I did for a living. Usually it was just polite nods and 'where do you work when you're not writing?' He reached out a hand. "I'm Ian."

I was tempted to say that I'd already known his name but there wasn't any way of saying it without him thinking that I'd been asking questions about him. I had been, but he didn't need to know that.

"Beth." I shook his hand. That small touch made me wish that he was touching other parts of me and not just with his hand. I'd never had this kind of reaction before and I didn't know how to deal with it.

"Do you want to come in, maybe have a cup of coffee?"

The invitation is tempting and when I shook my head, I saw a look of confusion cross his face for a split second before it vanished off of his beautiful features. "I would love to but I'm a little busy. I lost an hour today so I need to catch up on some work."

"How about later? Come around any time. I work from home too."

"I wouldn't want to be interrupting anything." God, how embarrassing would it be to knock on the door and have it answered by one of the harem of women he seemed to entertain.

He shrugged, a careless move of the shoulder. "It isn't going to be a problem."

I didn't know how to answer that, so I smiled softly and headed back to my flat. There was no way that I'd go up there again. That man looked like trouble with a capital T and I had no interest in becoming another notch in his bedpost.

I said the words over and over but it didn't sound any truer the more I said it. I wanted that man so bad I could already taste him under my lips.

Ian was true to his word, and there weren't any more loud girls visiting his flat. Actually, for a while I thought that he'd gone somewhere else. It was blissfully quiet and I enjoyed every minute of it. Okay, I didn't enjoy every minute. There was this dark little voice in the back of my mind that was urging me to go upstairs and take that cup of coffee he'd offered. Something about him intrigued the hell out of me. I wasn't sure if it was the writer part of me, or the woman, although it was probably a mixture of the two.

My first cup of coffee of the day tasted heavenly. I'd managed to hit most of my deadlines last night, but it had been a late one and I'd slept in. I pulled back the curtains and let the light shine in. It promised to be a beautiful day.

A knock at the door interrupted my planning for the day and, in my very cute bunny slippers, I went to answer it. Ian was leaning against the doorframe. Did he think that he was just too cool to stand unaided? Dark hair fell in front of dark eyes. He was wearing the black long sleeved top and pants again but he was now wearing black shoes. It wouldn't surprise me if everything in his wardrobe was black.

"Ian, what are you doing here?"

"I thought that maybe you'd want to do something. I have a free day, I know that you don't go out much, and I thought I'd offer to show you around town."

"Okay." The word was out of my mouth before I could even think to stop it.

That bemused expression was back. "I thought that you'd take more time deciding. I had a whole speech planned out and everything."

"I was just wondering what I was going to do today. I'd like to go out. Want to go back upstairs and wait for me to get changed?" I'd never been like this before. Ian was sexy as hell and I'd never been comfortable talking to somebody so out of my league. Although I might be shy, I wasn't stupid. This was going to be the ideal time to find out more about the mysterious man that lived above me.

"Can't I wait for you here?"

"No, I'll knock on your door when I finish getting dressed." I closed the door in his face, but before it closed I caught a faint look of surprise. He probably wasn't used to having doors shut in his face, though if he'd been half naked, it probably would have been a very different story. I might've been shy but I sure as hell wasn't a saint.

It didn't take me very long to grab some clothes and get dressed. I didn't want to look like I was making too much of an effort but I also didn't want to look boring. That just left a pair of dark blue jeans and a white top, which was sleeveless and had a peter pan collar. It looked great against my dark skin and I gave myself a sly wink as I checked out my reflection in the mirror. I didn't know what it was about Ian that I found so damn appealing, besides the fact he wasn't my type at all. He was a player and I'd never found that sexy before.

I plucked my leather jacket off the coat stand I'd placed by the front door, picked up my keys, and stopped short as I opened the door.

"Have you been waiting here all this time?"

Ian got to his feet, and as he brushed off his jeans, I got busy checking him out. I fought the urge to grab him by his top and drag him into my flat. I wasn't normally like this but something about him called out to the primal side of me.

"Yeah, well there wasn't much point going back upstairs." He glanced up toward his flat and I caught a look I'd never seen before and certainly one that I didn't think he even knew he had. He was nervous, interesting.

"Who are you hiding from?" I can't help the teasing edge to my words or the slow grin that was threatening to take over my face.

He looked back at me and graced me with another one of those lazy smiles. "Well aren't you the observant one." He reached out, grabbed my hand and started to pull me to the stairs. I heard a noise that sounded like someone was knocking on his door upstairs. "Come on, we better hurry." And we were off.

We ended up a few blocks away from the apartments in a small coffee shop. I noticed that a lot of the girls checked him out but Ian didn't even look at them. I guess it would be a different story if I wasn't there. We sat down at a table and he plucked up one of the menus, opened it up and placed it so it obscured the table and he ducked down slightly.

"Seriously, who are you hiding from?"

"Nobody important. Give it a few hours and it will be safe to go back."

"You never struck me as being somebody who'd hide away from their problems."

He shrugged. "Well this girl is persistent."

I looked around the coffee shop. "I'm sure she won't find us here. You can probably stop hiding."

"I'm not hiding."

I laughed, I couldn't help it. This strong and powerful man was doing anything but that. Okay, he was still sexy but somehow he'd become accessible. The wall that he seemed to have around himself the first couple of times I'd seen him had vanished. He looked a little bewildered but soon he followed me in a very manly laugh that did interesting things to my body. Our drinks arrived, a cup of coffee for him and tea for me. I took my first sip and then said what I'd been thinking about for a while.

"What do you do?"

He raised an eyebrow. "What do you think I do?"

I put the cup down and absent-mindedly ran my fingertips over the lip of the cup. "Well I have several theories. Michelle, the lady downstairs got me thinking that you were an escort." I was surprised at my forwardness but by the look on Ian's face he didn't seem to mind.

"I'm not an escort. Are you disappointed?"

"If you were, I'm pretty sure that I wouldn't be able to afford you."

He raised an eyebrow. "And why is that?"

Because you're so good looking that you could charge any price and somebody would always be willing to pay it. "I'm not here to stroke your ego."

He leaned forward and I caught a smell of his aftershave. My mouth suddenly became wet and it wasn't the only part of me.

"What do you want to stroke?" He said the words low and they seemed to rumble in his chest and caress my skin.

I shook my head, trying to focus on something besides him. I picked up the menu and tried to read it. "God, is there ever a time when you don't flirt?"

He leaned back again and smiled. "It's second nature."

"Well it doesn't work on me."

"Liar." He winked at me before plucking the menu out of my hands and calling a waitress over. He took one look at me, then the menu, and then ordered strawberry cheesecake. The waitress blushed and I couldn't blame her. Ian was having the same effect on me.

"You could have asked me what I wanted."

"What's the point in that? You'd take one look at the menu and decide that you couldn't actually have anything because of some reason or another." With one arm seeming to hold the curve of the table and another one placed just under his chin, it looked like he was studying me and he didn't bother to hide it. "I just took control."

I hated to admit it but he was right. I probably wouldn't have ordered off the menu. Being a writer meant I never seemed to get enough exercise. If I wasn't careful the weight would creep on and it would be hard to shake off again. "Do you do that often?"

"What?"

"Take control?"

"In every situation it matters." He bit his finger, a small nip and for a second I forgot how to breathe. He never took his eyes off of me.

"You never did answer my question about what you do for a living."

"You're right. I didn't."

We didn't seem to talk about anything vitally important and in the end I didn't learn anything new about Ian except that he liked to read. I asked him if he ever planned to write about his exploits but he didn't answer me, just gave me a knowing smile. After we finished the dessert, which we shared, he paid for the coffees and the dessert. It felt a little like a date but I knew that it wasn't, well a part of me knew that it wasn't.

We got our coats and headed back to the apartment. "Thanks for the afternoon out, I really needed a change of scenery."

"And thank you for the nice change of pace," he said as he walked me to my door. He reached into his pocket and pulled out a card. "If you're ever interested in finding out what I do for a living, feel free to come upstairs and I'll show you."

I took the card and read, Ian Gild: Photographer. "What kind of photographer?"

"You'll have to come upstairs to find out."

I had every intention of throwing away his card. Instead I put a pin through it and attached it to my bulletin board. Since I'd placed the board right next to the computer, I saw it every time I logged on. I was strong; I waited two weeks before I unpinned it and took a long hard look at it. It really gave me no clues to what he did up there, though I did have a few ideas of my own. I twirled the white card between my fingers and then placed it between my lips as I thought about his offer.

You'll have to come upstairs to find out.

He seemed like a nice enough guy, but that didn't matter much in the long run. An element of him just seemed to scream dark and mysterious. I really hadn't learned anything about him in the café. He'd managed to dodge and weave around my questions like a true man of mystery.

I got to my feet, slipped his card into my back pocket and went to find my shoes. It was probably a really bad idea but the curiosity was killing me. I had to find out what he did up there.

My heart was going a mile a minute, but I took the steps slowly. What if he had someone up there? What if the offer to show me what he did was off the table? I mean, it had been two weeks. I hadn't heard from him, and the flat upstairs had been quiet. I barely heard him moving up there at all. Not that I was intentionally listening for him. My words sounded false even to me. I hadn't been able to get Ian out of my head. He'd ended up taking center stage in a few of my more personal fantasies.

I rubbed my slightly sweaty hands

against the seat of my jeans. I didn't have to knock on his door, I could just turn around and head back to the safety of my room. I was just about to head back down the stairs when the door behind me opened.

"Beth?"

Crap. I turned around and was greeted by the sight that was Ian. It might have been the middle of the day but it looked like Ian had just gotten out of bed. He'd managed to pull a shirt on, but left open to reveal washboard abs. His jeans were loose, and long enough to brush the tops of his bare feet. The black hair was a mess but damn if it didn't look good on him.

"I'm sorry, I didn't think you'd still be in bed."

He opened the door further. "I had a late night. Come in, I was just about to make coffee. Do you want one?"

"Okay." I walked the rest of the way up the stairs, passed him and nearly stopped. His flat wasn't what I'd been expecting at all, but then I wasn't entirely sure what I'd been expecting. It looked normal; maybe I'd been expecting a typical bachelor's pad. In fact it looked a little like mine, but better decorated.

"Are you just going to stand there? The kitchen's through the door on your left." His words weren't even dirty but they still made me blush like a school girl.

Thankfully he was still behind me and he missed the sight of my cheeks going red.

I hopped onto one of the chairs around the high kitchen table and watched as Ian made the coffee.

"You've got a lot of self-control." His words seemed to just come out of the blue and brought my attention away from his finely toned ass.

"What do you mean?"

"It took you two weeks to come up here. Most girls it only takes five minutes."

"What do you do?" Come on, tell me, I silently begged. "You invite girls up here but you're not an escort. I'd heard some of the girls from my room. Whatever you do they certainly enjoy it."

He turned around and leaned across the kitchen counter. "And do you want me to do the same to you?"

"I want some answers." And for you to make love to me on the kitchen table. I couldn't help the look I give him. He had to know how much I wanted him.

"I don't owe you answers," he said stubbornly.

"No you don't, but you gave me the card. I thought you wanted to tell me."

He uncrossed his arms, the coffee forgotten behind him. He looked all coiled up with energy. "I don't want to tell you, I want to show you." He walked around the table, getting close to me with every step

117

that he took.

Suddenly I was nervous. I knew that I should have stayed downstairs, played it safe in my room and forgotten about him. Then he reached out, into my hair and unclipped the dark locks. The weight of it against my back was comforting, but soon his fingers were threaded through the dark strands. I still hadn't moved, I didn't want to, a little afraid that it might break the spell that he seemed to have woven over me.

His other hand came to my face, turning it slightly. Our eyes locked. "Do you trust me?"

I shouldn't, I knew that I shouldn't, but it was like my body has gone into autopilot. He picked up my hand and I hopped off the chair and let him lead me gods know where. We went through the living room, past a bedroom and into a studio.

"You're an S&M photographer?"

I just couldn't get my head around it. It made sense, I mean, why else would a photographer have that much leather and PVC? I guessed that it made a sort of twisted sense that he'd end up having sex with a few of his models. There was something so sexy about being tied up and having your picture taken.

I wondered what it would feel like kneeling in front of him, letting him tie me up. I knew that he would be forceful, he was used to taking control, and the thought made me wet with desire. I walked around the table, curiosity firmly taking hold as I studied everything. I traced my hand over the instruments and as I moved my fingers over the blindfold, I picked it up.

The material was smooth and soft in my hand and I looked over my shoulder at Ian. He was studying me from the doorway. "I'd love to know what it feels like."

He raised his eyebrow. "Are you sure?" He walked towards me. "It's a powerful feeling, being tied up. It usually calls to people who have a need to let go, to pass on the control to somebody else. Why do you want to do this?"

I couldn't help the smile that graced my lips. "Let's just call it research."

"That's not really a good enough reason. I need honesty."

I took a deep breath. "I want to put myself in your hands. I need to feel myself in your hands. There is something about you that calls to me. I think on some level we understand each other."

A slow smile graced his lips. "I think you're right." There was something animalistic about him that should have scared me but it didn't. "Being tied up means putting absolute trust in the person who ties you up." He reached out, brushing his fingertips against my cheek. "So the real question is, do you trust me?"

It wasn't the first time he'd asked me. I did trust him. I'd seen the person he'd kept hidden beneath that cocky layer. God, I wanted him, and this was a game that we could play for a while. We could each push each other to our limits. He could help me discover parts of me that I didn't even know existed.

"Yes I do."

He smiled approvingly. "Then we'll start with the blindfold." He offered me his hand and I slipped mine into it. With his other hand he pulled the blindfold out of my hand and it slipped through my fingertips.

"You might want to get comfortable. Take off your jacket and your shoes." I followed his instructions. I loved how he controlled this situation, how he was controlling me. "I'm not going to take any pictures, so you don't have to worry about that. Kneel down, center of the floor." He pointed at where he wanted me. I slipped my shoes and jacket off, and handed them to Ian. He went to leave them by the door and I knelt down on the floor.

"You know, you can tie my hands up. So I get the full range of experiences."

He smiled at me and winked. "Shh, just put yourself in my capable hands." He stepped behind me and knelt. With gentle hands on my shoulders, he moved me until I was up on my knees. I could feel his whole body pressed against mine. I fought the urge to roll my hips, to feel another part of him pressed against me. He draped the blindfold over my shoulder, reached across the front of me and drew the soft fabric against my chest. I watched as Ian raised it in front of me and it covered my eyes. With quick strokes, he tied it with practiced ease.

"Can you see anything?" I shook my head. "If at any time you want to stop, say Rose. It's a safety word and as soon as you say it, I'll stop."

"And if I don't want you to stop?" There was something so freeing about not being able to see and I took full advantage of it by being bold for a change.

"Then I'll take this as far as you want it to go."

How had this happened? How did I go from walking up those stairs, to trying to find out what he did for a living, to thinking about sex or having that promise of sex? Ian stood up behind me and by putting a slight pressure to my shoulders, guided me to sit down.

I listened as he walked away from me, probably towards the table. I wondered what he was going to pick up.

"This is a good place to start," he said

slowly and then suddenly he was back in front of me. It surprised me how my other senses seemed to be working at a higher level. All I could smell was him. "Lay down Beth."

I followed his instructions, curious to what he would do to me. "Can you feel this?" Something soft brushed my arm and I nodded. "What do you think it is?"

"A feather?" I guessed.

He brushed it up my arm, across my lips and down my other arm. I didn't think it would be like this. I thought it would be darker, but this was almost chaste, an innocent game. "Is this what you do with your models?"

"No, but this is what I do if I'm introducing someone to the S&M world. It's a powerful world to be introduced to. If it's handled in the wrong way, it will scare you. It shouldn't. You're an interesting girl, and I'm not even sure you know how powerful you are."

"How am I powerful?" Nobody had ever described me like that.

"Because nobody has had the effect on me as you have."

I bit my lip. "And what effect is that?"

I felt him as he laid down next to me. He traced my body with his fingertips, the curve of my lip, a sensitive part behind my ear. The simple touches made my heart race. What would he do next?

He started to undo the buttons on my shirt. Cold air touched my skin, quickly followed by his fingers again. The gentle assault of pleasure seemed to take forever and my body was starting to ache. He flipped open the buttons on my jeans and my heart stopped.

He hadn't even kissed me yet and I was already wet for him. As if he read my thoughts, I felt a brush of his lips against me. I couldn't help the sigh of pleasure that escaped me. I heard a rustle of clothes being removed and suddenly wished that I could see him. I knew that every inch of him would be beautiful.

Ian started slowly, agonizingly slow. He played with my body, then pushed a finger into me and I cried out in delight.

"Do you like how I touch you?"

"Yes."

"And when I do this?" He worked the finger in and out, and with his thumb he rubbed my clit.

"I really like that." I was breathing heavily. My body felt like it was seeking something and I know what it was. I didn't want to come over Ian's hand, I wanted him inside of me.

"What else do you want?"

I took a deep breath but the ways his fingers were playing with me was distracting as hell. "I want you. I want you inside of me."

He flexed his finger. "I am inside of you. What part of me do you want inside of you? Let me hear you say it, Beth."

"Your cock, I want to come over your hard cock."

His lips suddenly were pressed against my forehead. "Whatever the lady wishes." It was hard to believe that I hadn't moved from where I'd been first laid on the floor. He pulled my jeans all of the way off and nudged my legs apart.

"Wait."

He stopped. "What's wrong?"

I pulled the blindfold off. The light was a little harsh to my eyes. Ian's widened in surprise. "No more research?"

I flipped the makeshift blindfold over his head, and using the ends, I pulled him towards me, kissing him with renewed passion. I took control and the groan that came from his lips made me think that he liked it. He rubbed his cock over my clit and suddenly I was coming in waves, finally finding release. I didn't scream but I nipped his shoulder. Then he pushed inside of me. I opened my eyes and realized that Ian was looking at me intently. There was a thin layer of sweat on his forehead. He had himself under such a tight leash of control.

I bucked my hips, nipping at his lips. I wanted to feel him losing control and I used all the weapons in my arsenal. He smiled at me and then started to fuck me the way I wanted him to. We seemed to disappear in a mix of kissing and thrusts, groans and moans. I knew the instant that he was going to come, his breath became edgy as if he was about to finish a long race and then he roared. The one pure moment sent me spiraling into another orgasm. My mind went blissfully blank and then Ian slumped over me.

"I've never lost control like that before." I could hear the disbelief in his voice and I smiled.

"Stick with me kid, I could show you so much more."

He laughed. "Are you teasing me?"

I joined in. "I think you can handle it."

6 THE BILLIONAIRE

This was the part of her day she hated. Helena Bryce stood in the line and impatiently tapped her foot. If she only had a decent coffee machine in her office, it would save her so much time and energy, but no, she had never bothered to spend the extra money. It had a bright side though. While it might annoy her, she could add it to her weekly exercise routine. It was quite a walk in a pair of high heels.

It wouldn't annoy her so much if she didn't have a business meeting that was starting in half an hour. She usually trusted her assistant, Kelly, to get all her things together, but there was something about this meeting that was rubbing her the wrong way. Helena ran a PR company, she'd always been a people person, and she brought her own skill and flair to the job. The company she was meeting with today, Endgame, specialized in computer games, and while it was still small in the world of computers, it had the potential to be huge. Unfortunately, that was just about all she knew about it. She hated going into a meeting blind, but the company head was being greedy with information. It was like the owner was trying to surprise her, to keep her off balance.

"Are you having the usual, Ms. Bryce?" Helena looked up and into the eyes of the young coffee seller. She'd never bothered to learn his name, since there really wasn't much point. The faces in this place changed with surprising regularity.

She nodded and popped her credit card into the machine, quickly typing in her pin number. She didn't have long to wait before the latte with a shot of caramel was ready and waiting for her. Helena nodded her thanks to the server and made her way to work.

Today was either going to go really well or really badly, and she wished she knew what to expect. She was known for her knowledge. You didn't get far in the world of PR if you didn't know everyone or at least know someone who knew someone else. Helena had gotten Kelly to ask all their usual leads for information, but nothing panned out. Endgame seemed to be shrouded in mystery and Helena hated a mystery.

"Okay, what do you have, Kelly?"

Kelly seemed to burst into action as soon as Helena walked into the office. "I'm so sorry Helena, they arrived early, and I couldn't get you on the phone. Duncan's sorting out coffee for them and I put them in the conference room."

"Remember to breathe, Kelly." Okay, this day was already down the crapper. Helena shrugged out of her jacket and took the file that Kelly offered her. She ran her fingers through her hair and took a deep breath that helped steady and focus her mind.

"It's okay, Kelly. Sit in on the meeting and take some notes."

Kelly quickly moved to her desk and retrieved her notepad. Helena waited a brief second before heading to the conference room. She gave the folder a quick look through, but there wasn't anything in it she didn't already know.

She pushed open the door. "Good morning, I'm sorry that I'm late. I wasn't expecting you to arrive so early." She looked up, officially getting the first look at her new clients and suddenly, she forgot how to breathe.

She hadn't seen him since high school. He looked taller, which was strange considering he was sitting down. The suit looked expensive and it was something she wouldn't have expected from him.

"Steven Carter," she greeted. It wasn't much of a hello, but she hated the fact he had an unfair advantage. He obviously knew who she was before approaching the company. She, on the other hand, had been taken completely unaware. It didn't sit well with her.

She looked beautiful and powerful, but he'd caught the surprise that briefly showed in her eyes. He knew how he looked and he wanted to start this meeting off on the right foot. He wasn't the boy she knew from school. He was a billionaire.

The computer games that he'd worked on for years had been picked up by a company and become downloadable to phones. Then he'd struck out on his own and while his company was small, he'd invested well. The next logical step was to get his face out there and he knew that Helena's company was the best place to start.

It had also been impossible to resist seeing her again. Back in high school, they'd run in completely different circles, the geek and the popular girl. She'd never looked at him but he'd worshipped her from afar.

He let Arthur, his lawyer, handle the conversation. He kept his eyes on Helena. Damn, she was beautiful. Her dark hair had been clipped up and the red skirt she wore clung to well-shaped hips. She wore a black shirt and the way it enhanced her breasts nearly made his mouth water.

"This is a more detailed view of the company and where Mr. Carter wants to take it over the next five years. There are also plans to set up a fund for talented youth who might want a career in this industry."

Helena looked over at Steven and his mouth went dry. "Interesting, that's something I can work with."

They talked over a few more things but Steven only half listened. Arthur would fill in the details later. He wondered what it would be like to kiss her. He'd had his high school fantasies and plenty of hot dreams about her. He wondered if she'd live up to those dreams. As soon as the meeting was finished, Arthur flipped open his phone and promptly vanished to make a call. Helena's assistant left promptly to type up the notes of the meeting.

"I'll have my team look over the information and we'll put a plan together. I'll need a few weeks, will that be alright?"

"That'll be fine," Steven said, the first words he'd spoken since the meeting started. Helena looked at him.

"So you do speak." Her tone was teasing and Steven smiled at her.

"I've been known to from time to time."

"So I'll call you if I have any questions?"

"Call me if you want anything." The words were heavy with meaning and Helena's eyes widened in surprise.

"I don't mix business with pleasure."

He raised his eyebrow and looked her up and down. The smile that crossed his face was utterly manly. "That's a shame."

Helena hadn't been able to stop thinking about Steven since he'd left her office. He was living proof that high school didn't mean anything. He was probably the last person she would have expected to become one of the youngest billionaires in the UK. It became a lot easier to get information about him once she had a name.

They'd run in completely different groups and Steven had been the target of a few of her friends' jokes. They hadn't been nice jokes and in hindsight, Helena didn't know why she'd hung out with them.

She sat on her sofa. The TV was on but the volume was low and she wasn't really paying attention to it. She sipped at a glass of red wine and studied his card. He'd actually come on to her. She had read the signs and the whole 'call me if you need anything' line was pretty obvious. It didn't really surprise her that Steven had the confidence that he lacked in high school. Lots of money could do that.

Helena was surprised that she was a little interested in his offer. She would never mix business with pleasure but in this case, she was tempted. It wasn't even the money; she had a healthy stock portfolio and the business was doing well. Still, she was intrigued.

She brought the card to her lips and remembered how Steven had rubbed his bottom lip. She'd seen more than her share of good-looking men, but none of them had gotten under her skin as he had.

Helena had a little more wine and picked up her phone. She dialed the number quickly before she could stop herself from making one of those mistakes that you could never take back.

"Hello, Helena."

"How did you know it was me?"

Steven laughed and the sound of his voice traveled through the phone and tickled her spine. "I didn't, but I hoped that you would call. What can I do for you?"

Bend me over the table in my living room and do things to me that will make my toes curl? Helena took a deep breath. "It was a surprise seeing you today. Did you know that I run the company you were using?"

She could hear the background sound of a busy road and it made her suspect that she'd caught him in his car. "Yes. In fact, the reason you run it was the reason I wanted to work with it."

That was a forwardness that Helena liked. "And why did you want to work with me?"

Steven sighed and Helena got the impression that he wasn't impressed but her question. "I've thought a lot about you since leaving school. I'm happy to see that you did so well for yourself. Now, why did you really call at eleven at night?"

"I wanted to know if the offer to help me with anything was still on the table." She held her breath. She was being submissive, and while it wasn't a natural feeling or emotion to her, Steven brought it out in her. She wasn't sure if she liked it or not.

"I'll be there in ten minutes."

The phone went dead in her hand and she darted off to make herself look a little more presentable. God, it felt like she was back in high school again. She'd had plenty of lovers since then but this was the first time she had butterflies in the pit of her stomach.

This was a really bad idea, Steven knew it but by the way his hard cock made a tent of his trousers, his cock was certainly not being controlled by his brain tonight. There had been a part of him, a logical part of his brain, that had been sure she wouldn't call. And even if she did, she wouldn't be asking for what he assumed she was asking for.

This was starting to get complicated. He nodded at his driver and George took it as a cue to head to Helena's house.

She was nervous. Her heart had taken up permanent residence in her throat and was beating so loud that it felt like her head was vibrating. She downed the glass of wine, hoping that the sweet liquid would help to calm her down. It worked a little.

Then there was a knock on the door.

She quickly went to answer it and was swept up in Steven's arms and kissed so thoroughly that it left her breathless and hot.

"I really hope that's what you wanted or this has gotten off on the wrong foot."

His words made her laugh a little and she suddenly felt a lot more relaxed. "Yeah, I definitely wanted that."

"Good." He cradled her face between his

hands and started to kiss her more thoroughly. "I've been thinking about that kiss since high school. I wanted it to be memorable."

Helena pulled away from his questing lips and he frowned at her, as if asking what was wrong. "You've wanted this since high school?"

Steven nodded and for a brief second he looked a lot like the boy she remembered from high school and she found it endearing. She went back to kissing him, removing his jacket and then his tie. "You know that this is a bad idea right?"

"You did say that you didn't mix business and pleasure," he agreed as he unzipped her skirt and let it fall to the living room floor. He groaned as his fingertips touched bare skin. "Damn you're so beautiful."

Helena grabbed a handful of his shirt and pulled him up. She had to make sure that they were clear on this. The fact that he thought that she was beautiful and had wanted this high school meant that this could get very complicated. "The only way that this will work is if it's only for one night."

Lust cleared from his eyes a little, though his hands hadn't traveled far from their resting place on her ass. "Are you serious?"

"Yes. Look, we're both very busy people.

Our companies mean the world to us and I can't be distracted from it." She wasn't sure what kind of answer that she expected from that but being lifted up into his arms, feeling muscles tighten as he held on to her, wasn't it.

"We'll talk about it in the morning," he promised. He hadn't expected that but if he made tonight memorable, something that stayed on her mind and made her think of him, then this could end up being something so much more. He'd loved her since high school, that hadn't changed in the time that he hadn't seen her and tonight wasn't going to change how he felt about her either.

He helped her out of her shirt and ran his hands over her silk chemise. He loved how it felt under his hands. He kissed her chest, brushing his lips against the rough lace detail at the top. Helena's head tipped back, obviously caught up in the sensations that he was creating.

"Where's your bedroom?"

Her head tipped forward and her face became half hidden behind a veil of dark hair. "It's the first door on the right upstairs."

Steven picked her up and carried her upstairs, barely breaking the kiss that seared his very soul. He sat her down on the bed and spread her legs, kneeling between them. She used her arms to brace herself as he pulled down her panties and slipped them off.

He loved the smell of her, that slightly musky scent that meant she was as turned on by this as he was. Her pussy glistened with juices and he dipped his head and delicately tasted her. He wanted to fuck her with his tongue and really enjoy everything about her but he took his time. His cock strained in his trousers and it demanded attention but would have to wait as well.

Steven flicked his tongue over her clit and was rewarded with a deep groan of satisfaction. He then started his assault on her cunt. The way her hand and fingertips laced through his dark hair drove him on and when she came in a gushing wave, he greedily lapped up her juices. He pushed a finger into her tight pussy and it glided in.

She was more than ready for him.

He got to his feet and Helena looked up at him with a slightly dazed look in her eyes. She leaned forward, undid his belt, and pulled it free with one deft flick of her hand. Steven reached out and cupped the side of her face; she winked at him as she undid his trousers and unleashed his cock. It was hard, wet at the tip, and more than ready.

"There are some condoms on the top shelf." Helena said, her voice thick with desire.

This time Steven smiled and it was filled with promise. "We don't need them just yet."

Damn, she needed him in her in the worst possible way. The way he'd licked her pussy had been absolutely amazing. Who knew someone who was a geek in high school could do something like that? She sure as hell hadn't.

He pushed her until she was lying on her bed and gently turned her around until they were spooning. He rested his cock between the curves of her ass and slowly started to kiss her neck. He slid his hand over the smooth planes of her stomach and started to play with her clit again.

The orgasm hit her from out of nowhere. Her clit was still sensitive and her whole body arched into his. She rolled her hips and his hot breath tickled her neck as she rubbed his cock. A nip on her earlobe stopped the gentle roll of her hips.

"If you keep doing that, this could be over in minutes. But I'm going to make love to you for hours, Helena. I'm going to make you come so hard that you see stars. And I'm going to make you beg for me to finish it and only then am I going to slip this hard cock into your wet pussy." The words were whispered hotly into her ear, and held such a wealth of promise.

He flipped her onto her back, a move so sudden that it took her completely by surprise. The weight of his body pressed down on hers, and to feel how aroused he was to be half lying on top of her felt incredible. She loved how he looked leaning over her, dark and intense. With only the bedside light on, it cast interesting shadows across his face. He dipped down and kissed her. The way he slowly pushed his tongue into her mouth hinted at what was going to come later. Their tongues battled and danced as her hands traveled over the rugged length of his body.

She was incredible; he loved the way she moaned as he played with her. He'd loss count of how many times he made her explode with desire. She was so responsive under his hands, and he felt like a mechanic making a car purr under expert hands.

He was going to have to push himself into her soon. His cock was throbbing and he gripped it with his hand.

"Please, Steven," she begged. Steven looked down and into the eyes that burnt with desire.

"Please what?"

"Please fuck me." Helena moved her knees and spread her legs. It was going to feel so good to slip into the wet and hot pussy. It had taken all of his self-control not to bury himself deep in her as soon as he'd arrived. But then the night would have been over before it truly began.

He pushed into her with agonizing slowness and she nearly went wild with need. Her whole body craved him and it amazed her that he'd dragged this out. It was like he was committing every part of her body to memory. She reached down with one hand and played with her clit as he slowly fucked her.

She rested her other hand on his chin, making sure not to break eye contact. Her body was sleek with sweat, and parts of it ached sweetly. The full length of his cock filled her in ways that she didn't think was possible. With her fingers teasing out even more pleasure, she could feel his abs tense as he worked in and out of her.

In that split second she knew that she was in trouble. She didn't want the night to end.

His thrusts became faster and she knew he was about to come. As soon as that happened, it would end. She said that they had one night together. Would he leave after this? Suddenly her mind went blissfully blank as her orgasm quickly followed his and he half collapsed on top of her.

They both struggled to catch their breath and half smiled at each other.

"I don't think I could have imagined it

any better than that." His words made her smile as they slowly disengaged. "Is it okay if I sleep here?"

"I don't think that's a good idea. We did agree on one night." As soon as the words left her lips she wished that she could have taken them back.

Steven's eyes darken for a split second and she was sure it wasn't from renewed desire. "Good point. I should be going then."

This wasn't good. It didn't feel right pushing him away after what they'd shared. "You don't have to go right away. Do you want coffee or something?"

Steven visibly relaxed. "I'd like that."

They talked into the early morning. They joked about school and how their worlds had turned out. It surprised her how easy it was to talk to him. She thought that the conversation would be stilted and uncomfortable after he'd seen her at her most vulnerable. They'd ended up falling asleep on the couch together, her chin resting on his chest.

When she woke up the next morning he was gone. All he left was a note, a time and a place. That was it.

She couldn't help the smile that unfolded on her face.

Steven arrived home and stepped into the shower. He had no idea if Helena would read the note, but desperately hoped she'd come.

He looked in his wardrobe, a towel wrapped around his waist and beads of water still on his skin. He gazed longingly at the jeans, T-shirts and casual shirts. It had been mostly Arthur's idea that he brought the suits. A professional meeting meant a professional look, at least that was what Arthur had said.

Steven was probably going to have to mention at some point why he never wore a suit again after the business part of it was concluded. He called his driver after he'd finished getting dressed and then gave him six months wages to let him borrow the car. He could have probably just asked but it was a just in case he broke it. He had a license of course, but driving wasn't really in his area of expertise.

Though when they met, he wouldn't have to drive very far. They needed to talk, so he planned to pick her up and take her to a restaurant. Then it would be time for some honesty. He had to be sure that she knew what he felt. He didn't just want to have sex with her; he wanted to be with her.

He'd tell her when he picked her up.

"I hadn't been expecting that," he laughed.

Helena looked down at him and smiled. As soon as they got somewhere quiet and deserted, Helena had told him to pull over. With a lot of giggling, they had ended up in the back seat, where she'd straddled him. Then their laughter had stopped and the heavy moans had started. She'd always thought that the back windows steaming up only happened in the movies, but their frosted windows proved that theory wrong.

"I thought that was why you left the note?"

Steven frowned. "I left the note so we could talk. Don't take me wrong, this was nice, but it wasn't why I left the note."

Helena started to sort out her clothes, readjusting her skirt back down over her hips and leaned over Steven and opened the back door, letting in some fresh air. "What's there to talk about?"

He straightened out his pants. "We need to talk about us."

The pause that followed was thick and heavy. Helena got off of his lap and sat down next to him in the back seat. "We agreed last night that it was only going to be one time."

"No, you said that it was going to be one night but look at us now. We've just had sex in my car, what does that mean?"

She wasn't sure what she should say. There was a part of her that wanted more but there was also a part that knew that it was impossible. They had nothing in common, they hadn't in high school, and they didn't now. This was why she didn't mixed business and pleasure, everything got complicated.

He makes you laugh, though, a tiny voice in Helena head whispered, when was the last time you laughed like that?

It didn't matter. She suppressed her longing and made up her mind.

"This was a mistake."

"Excuse me?"

"This is the reason I don't mix business with pleasure. I told you that I didn't, that it was a bad idea." She got out of the car. "I thought we had an understanding. I thought that we were both focused on our companies."

"Where are you going?"

"To work," she said as she turned around.

"We're in the middle of nowhere, Helena."

"Then I'll call a taxi," she called over her shoulder.

They hadn't talked since the argument. Helena had been knee deep in work and Steven had his company to manage. The stupid disagreement they had in the car still preyed on Steven's mind. He was in love with her, but maybe it had just been about the sex with her.

He stared blankly at the laptop screen and closed it with a resounding thud. He had all this money and the one woman he wanted didn't want anything from him. This was frustrating and annoying as hell.

He knew he had to let her go and move on. But there was still just one more thing that he could do.

He could tell her the truth.

Helena hadn't been able to think straight since the argument in the car. She'd shifted the majority of the work for Steven's company onto her assistant. Kelly had visibly paled when she'd handed her the folder, and promised her that if she did a good job on the account she'd get more work.

Kelly had looked at her like she'd lost her mind. Helena thought that she might have. How she had managed to screw up a relationship with Steven, she didn't know. It made no sense. The instant he'd talked about going out on an official date, she should have said yes. Instead they'd had an argument and the relationship had ended before it had begun.

She missed him. Not for the sex, which had been the best she'd ever had, but the way he made her feel: loved and desired. She rested her hand on her forehand and closed her eyes. They'd be making a presentation on Friday and then it would be last she'd see him.

She didn't think seeing him again was going to be easy in the slightest. Saying goodbye was going to be harder.

Friday came a lot more quickly than she thought possible. When she walked into the conference room she was anticipating seeing Steven waiting for her. She was a disappointed to see that he wasn't there and his lawyer was. Helena vaguely remembered that his name was Arthur, which was confirmed when he introduced himself again.

"Is Mr. Carter not attending today?"

"He got called away on other matters. There's no need to worry, Steven has a great deal of faith in my judgment."

"Well that's good to hear. The presentation will start in a few moments. If you'll excuse me, I have to go and make a quick phone call."

She was crushed and while she knew why, she didn't know why she was surprised. There was really no reason for

Steven to be at this meeting. She quickly walked into her office, closing the door behind her and leaned her back against it.

Helena didn't bother to try and stop the tears. She could call him, she wanted to, but she didn't know what to say. It was too late. She was too late.

"Why are you crying?" Steven's voice asked, startling her.

She stared at him in disbelief. "Christ, Steven. What the hell are you doing in here?" She wiped the tears away, wishing she could hide them.

The sight of the man who occupied her thoughts, who'd made her cry like a heartbroken girl, made her heart skip a beat. He was sitting in her chair and he looked a little unsettled by the fact she was crying.

"I thought Arthur said that you were too busy to attend?"

"I needed to talk to you." He slowly got to his feet. He wasn't wearing a suit today and he looked comfortable, normal. It was a look that she liked on him. "Damn, I've played this conversation a million times in my head but now you're in front of me? I don't know what to say."

Is it possible to forget how to breathe? Helena couldn't move from her spot just in front of the door.

"The thing is, Helena, I've been in love with you since high school and I'm still in love with you. In all honesty, the suits and the flashy cars aren't me. It was a look that I thought would attract you. The truth is I'm this," he gestured to his jeans and shirt as he walked toward her, "I was just a gamer that got incredibly lucky and I wanted to share that luck with others. If we're going to work as a couple, I needed to be honest with you." He hadn't stopped walking until he stopped in front of her. "And judging by your reaction of thinking I wasn't here, I think you love me too. Am I wrong?"

Helena shook her head. "You're not wrong, Steven."

His movements were slightly hesitant as he reached up and touched her cheek. "Then how about a clean slate. What do you think about starting over?"

"That sounds perfect."

AUTHOR'S NOTE

Readers: I want to expand a few of the stories to see where the characters can be explored further. If there are any of the stories that you would like to read more about again, I'd love to hear from you!

Visit my blog at www.carricemckelvy.com

Join my newsletter for free exclusive previews
www.carricemckelvy.com/in

Follow me on Twitter at
www.twitter.com/carricemckelvy

Like my page on Facebook at
www.facebook.com/carricemckelvy

Discover my books at major ebook retailers everywhere.

Printed in Great Britain
by Amazon